Sassafras Land

Sassafras Land

A Tale of Redemption Among the Delaware

Robert M. Farrington

iUniverse, Inc.

New York Lincoln Shanghai

Sassafras Land
A Tale of Redemption Among the Delaware

iUniverse books may be ordered through booksellers or by contacting:

iUniverse
2021 Pine Lake Road, Suite 100
Lincoln, NE 68512
www.iuniverse.com
1-800-Authors (1-800-288-4677)

Because of the dynamic nature of the Internet, any Web addresses or links contained in this book may have changed since publication and may no longer be valid.

Certain characters in this work are historical figures, and certain events portrayed did take place. However, this is a work of fiction. All of the other characters, names, and events as well as all places, incidents, organizations, and dialogue in this novel are either the products of the author's imagination or are used fictitiously.

ISBN: 978-0-595-48007-4 (pbk)
ISBN: 978-0-595-60110-3 (ebk)

Printed in the United States of America

I dedicate this tale to the Indian peoples who understand the nature of our brief stay here on Mother Earth--that we must honor her gifts to us and protect her—and to Ray, who believed in my work and who showed me the way.

PREFACE

Slowly I drove by the overgrown graveyard—what remained of the Ballard family cemetery, dating back to the early eighteenth century. I recalled reading a local history of the colonial burial grounds and that the Ballard homestead had stood nearby. Many times I had passed by the marker, barely visible from the road, never taking a second look. But on that hot day, it stood apart from the tall weeds, alone on the top of a small hill, beckoning me. Pulling over, I hopped out of my car, making my way through the thick grass toward the marker, carefully avoiding the flourishing poison ivy vines and their toxic resin. Those excruciatingly itchy welts lay a brush of my bare ankles from the shiny deep green leaves. Approaching the marker, I pulled aside a single overhanging tree branch to reveal the fading words. Brushing away the sweat beads gathering on my brow, I squinted. The words danced before my eyes in the wilting July heat..... .1769.

1769—Canopus Hollow

The Tidd cabin stood in a hollow on the east end of the Highland Patent. The patent, stretching from Hudson's River to the west, was the most barren of any of the land found near this River of the Mountains. Squatters located here, left alone to farm, rent free. The landlords lived far off in New York City, indifferent to these hardy settlers scattered across their lands.

With his wife, Esther, and their infant child, Rebecca, Jacob Tidd arrived on the patent at Canopus Hollow, near Canopus Pond, shortly before the birth of their second child, Polly. As many of their Dutch predecessors still living nearby, they had emigrated from Long Island. Jacob, finding the hollow covered with dense forest and swamp, labored hard to clear an acre of the rocky soil, planting corn and potatoes. He built a log cabin and a shed, raised a yoke of steers, two milk cows, a half dozen sheep and kept a sheep dog to drive away the wolves and mountain lions roaming here in the shadow of the Hudson Highlands.

The dwelling was a story high with a stoop in front, the roof sloping to form the top of the stoop. The windows were small—glass was too expensive for larger ones—making the interior dark. The pine logs which Jacob had hauled from the surrounding forest were bare, the walls, unpainted, the floors laid with oak. One room dominated the entire structure, centering on a drafty fireplace, large enough to hold a half cord of wood.

The attic was finished barn style with shutters built into the gable at each end to admit light. It was within this dormer that Polly shared her sleeping quarters with Rebecca while their younger brother, Aaron, slept in a corner at the far end.

Surrounding the Tidd homestead was a stockade fence through which Jacob drove his sheep and cattle at night to protect them from beasts of prey or bands of plunderers called "cowboys," more feared than the Wappinger Indians living nearby.

Tachwoak! Bright, warm October morning. Jacob and Esther hitched their chestnut nag, Molly, to a crude two wheel cart, and climbed the rough mountain trail to their corn patch to harvest the remaining stand of corn. As they left, Jacob warned his three children, "Stay close to th' cabin. The men at th' mill toll me the'r skinners and cowboys on th' patent. A few bottles of whiskey in the'r gut— God only knows what they might do. Sarah'll warn you young uns 'gainst poachers. And Aaron! Remember my gun's armed an' ready standin' next to th' front door in easy reach."

"Yes, pa!" they chorused.

Like Polly, Aaron was big for his age, tall as his six foot father. He sported a crowd of red locks which fell to his shoulders, framing a round, freckled face. Aaron was quicker with a smile than his sisters who took after their stern mother, Esther.

Jacob, a man in his thirties, with a full, carrot-red beard, called back to the children as they disappeared up the trail.

"You young 'uns turn over th' piles of corn dryin' in th' front yard while yer ma an' me are workin' in th' corn patch."

His seven foot high stockade fence built of thick pine poles surrounded the yard, cabin and the shed where he kept his animals. After building the stockade, he had explained to the family, "This'll keep out the deer. They'd get in th' shed an' finish off a winter's stock of corn in a short night without th' fence to stop 'em and Sarah to drive 'em off."

From her bed in the shed, the sheep dog would alert them of any approaching strangers.

Earlier that morning, after breakfast, the three children sat at the Tidd's crude kitchen table, listening dutifully to Esther's reading of the Ninth Psalm from her tattered family Bible. Jacob mouthed the words after her, and then she asked each child to repeat a verse from memory. Although Polly was two years younger than Rebecca, her sharp memory and gifted voice sang out the inspiring words. It was Polly's favorite psalm, and later, as the three children set to work on their morning chores, the psalm resounded in her head as she carefully turned each brightly colored ear of corn in the drying patch of sunlight. She pictured King David working in the fields, David, the poet and warrior, joyfully praising the Lord.

His comforting words echoed on her lips.

"I thank you, O Lord, with all my heart. I shall recount all your wondrous deeds. I shall be glad and shall exult in you. I shall sing of your glory most High, because my enemies stumble and retreat; because they vanish before your presence."

King David, the righteous! She wondered if he sang those words just in the Temple, or whether he recited them at his work as she did, in the forest, and on Sunday mornings in the little Dutch church in nearby Fishkill where the Tidds went to worship. While Aaron and Rebecca gathered the ripe apples from beneath two scraggly apple trees, Polly sang the psalm in her alto voice. She gazed at the strong poles surrounding them. Pa was right! The apples would've long since been devoured by the deer without his stockade fence.

The warm autumn sun beat down on the three children as they shucked the ears of indian corn, its rays highlighting kernels of gold, yellow, and russet beads. Rebecca gathered the apples, placing them carefully in a wooden bucket while Aaron chased sluggish yellow jackets, drunk from the sweet apple nectar. As he brushed them away, they flew off lazily, only to return to alight on another pearl of the sticky resin.

Polly's carrot-red hair fell to her shoulders, her full bosom's cleavage visible above her flowered, cotton dress. Her skin was soft and white, her cheeks a blush—from working in her father's corn and potato patches and in the sunlit yard. Her eyes were large, round, and azure blue. When she smiled, they sparkled. Tall and buxom, she sometimes wished she were thinner, paler, more dainty, like Rebecca, or as gaunt and bony as Aaron.

One day, earlier that fall, after one of her walks down to Canopus Pond, she stood on its banks, shedding the dress and full petticoat that Esther had sown for her. Hiding the pile of clothes in the bushes, she slipped into the dark waters of the pond. Standing among the reeds and cattails, she gazed at her nakedness, silhouetted in the still water, admiring her full breasts and round hips. She thrust her torso forward, her ivory white breasts descending to pink, hard nipples, her plump buttocks exaggerating her reflection. She stood sideways, curious how she would look when she was grown—unaware that she already was. Then she leaped into the cool, refreshing arms of the pond, her skin and the red bush between her legs, marking a sharp contrast in the dark waters.

Later that afternoon, Polly sat on a log in the swamp, Bible in hand. Suddenly, blood trickled out from between her legs. She gasped, jumping to her feet, dropping the Bible. The blood ran down her smooth, creamy white thigh, gathering in a dimple, descending to a shapely knee.

Reaching beneath her petticoat, she withdrew her hand, revealing a thick red, oozing. Her cheeks paled as she plopped herself down on the log, the woods' green canopy hiding her.

"I must be goin' to bleed to death."

Squeezing her thighs together, she closed her eyes as if she were making an all-important wish. She drew the white folds of her petticoat up to her waist, her undergarment absorbing the sticky blood. The dampness of the cedar swamp rose up, invading her body. She whispered to herself.

"Becca told me such a thing'd happen to me one of these days."

But the start of Polly's womanhood lay, a distant star, far from her waking moments, or her dream-filled walks into the swamp in the morning after Bible reading and chores, and in the evening before prayers and more Bible reading.

Sun beams dropped through the canopy, lighting Polly's dimpled cheeks, her curly hair trailing down to her broad shoulders. She peered down between her legs.

"Mama never warned me such a thing'd come to pass."

She rose slowly from the log. Choking back sobs, lifting her petticoat and grasping the hem of the dress, she limped barefoot back to the cabin. On tiptoe, she slipped through the stockade gate. She fled to the privacy of the darkened shed. In the corner she found Sarah's empty bed, its soft, woolen blankets inviting her to lie down. She lay her buzzing head and aching body back against the thick, raw wool, musky sheep smell wafting up her nostrils. Her brain's insistent chatter resisted slumber. She finally cried herself to sleep

*   *   *   *

Mechkalanne sat cross legged on a boulder at a point where the Mahicanituk narrows, watching his brothers move swiftly away down river. The river was calm and placid, like a mirror. He spotted the four dugout canoes with their war party of twelve braves disappearing in a veil of mist. Their leader, Possum Eater's words echoed in the thin air.

"Mechkalanne will miss his chance to remove his petticoat and become a real Lenape—a true brave."

Mechkalanne looked down into the river spotting his own reflection. His head was shaved except for a crest across the top, braided in two scalp locks, one hanging forward, secured with a silver clasp, the other pitched to the back. His features, more angular and chiseled than the rounder faces of his brothers, revealed dark, piercing eyes. He was a head taller, his hard body, taut as a bowstring.

Possum Eater had called back to him.

"Mechkalanne fat and old, like squaws back at lodge."

His words rang hollow in the still morning air. And Mech's image in the still waters of the Mahicanituk told him this was not so.

The fog bank lifted. Mech's keen eyes scanned the river channel. Rounded mountains rose high on both sides, ablaze with oranges and reds splashed across a deep green—like sleeping bears they lay. The flotilla of canoes was only a distant speck in the widening river, the mountains falling away into a vast expanse of still water. The white men lived beyond these mountains and dense forest in a swampy area a sun's walk from the far side of the river. No Indian would dwell in such a place. The war party would be gone for two suns.

Possum Eater reminded his followers.

"The long knives braves will not see us as their forts stand many miles down river. We will find the squatters and kill them all. We will return with our war belts hanging with paleface scalps. This will prove we are not petticoated as our cousins, the *Mengwe*, have said."

Mechkalanne shed his deer skin leggings, removed his loin cloth and stood naked on the boulder, his tall, muscular body reflected on the water below. He dove into the clear, pristine river, plunging into its icy depths. There he spotted a sturgeon lumbering off into the deep of the narrow channel. The elusive white sturgeon, this great fish, reminded him of the story of the "Big Fish" of the palefaces that the Lenape's arrows and spears could not penetrate, the Big Fish on which the white man first appeared to his people, in which they had floated up the Great River of the North many summers earlier. So their grandfathers had told them.

The river chill penetrating him, Mechkalanne's long, lithe thigh muscles worked hard as he knifed down to the bottom, searching for fish eggs, his favorite delicacy. He forgot that it was *Tachwoak* and that the fish had long since left their spawn. His genitals, unprotected by the hug of the leather loincloth, shrank back into the warmth of his groin. The icy water resisted his powerful legs. Urging them to move faster, he frog kicked deeper into the river.

Moving effortlessly across the rock-strewn sandy bottom, he spotted an ancient snapping turtle treading water near a pointed boulder. It eyed him with a vacant stare, its hooked beak and powerful jaws warning him off. He smiled at the turtle, symbol of his clan, deciding that it had beaten him to his imagined newly spawned sturgeon eggs.

"I am swifter and keener of sight, but you are wiser, and this is your lodge."

He waved to the disappearing creature. His lungs ached. He pushed his big feet hard against the stone, jutting up from the river bottom, and shot up, the icy water sliding its wet hand across his naked body.

Breaking the mirrored surface, Mechkalanne spotted his former perch. Arching his buttocks and lower back, he pulled himself up onto the boulder. The sun's rays, cracking the mountain top, struck his shivering body. He dropped to his back, sprawled across the rock, his broad chest expanding. Exhaling deeply, he gazed at the cloudless sky.

The sun was higher now, its rays drying his copper body, glistening with pure water droplets from the *Mahicanituk*. As he drew in its warmth, his dark eyes swept across the broad sky, searching for his brother hawk, his namesake, and his cousin, the eagle, haunting the nearby mountains. His belly growled. Disappointed with his underwater hunt, he would fill his complaining stomach with tart cranberries, crabapples and roots from the nearby woods before returning to his village.

Mechkalanne lay on the rock, gazing at the endless sky above the *Mahicanituk*. He was eager to share with another the peace and joy in his heart. Rising, he quickly pulled on his loincloth, leggings, and deer skin moccasins for the journey back through the forest to his lodge and his people on the banks of the *Lenapewihituk*, the stream of the Lenape people. He would tell the sachem, Black Turtle, his adoptive father, of his decision to return to the village, of his wish not to accompany the war party pursuing the white squatters for their scalps. He knew that Black Turtle would nod his grey head, his long, thinning hair swaying back and forth, a sign that he had deliberated on Mech's decision, and had concluded that it was right and good.

The sachem's wisdom, like that of their totem, the Turtle, was deep, dark. His vision of Mother Earth/Turtle and his words were wise and simple. The young brave ran swiftly through the forest, his bright mind recalling Black Turtle's tale of why the Turtles, the members of the *Unami* clan, were the best. When Black Turtle spoke, he listened intently.

He pictured the sachem sitting at his fire, the Red Score sticks in his dark, wrinkled hands, gently fingering the notches on the red and black painted sticks. The old man would begin a tale told to him many winters earlier.

"White Turtle, my mother of earth and sky, told me this tale when I was but eight winters old. There were three creatures, man-like beings, the ones that began it all, the ones who created the totems of the Lenape. All three sat at their fire one cold winter night, arguing about which one was best. They finally agreed that each would tell his own story and then the sachem of the village would decide. He who told the best story would be judged the strongest, the wisest. So the turtle told his story first. It went like this.

'The Turkey, Wolf, and Turtle had an argument about which one was best. As they walked through the forest, they came to the *Mahicanituk*, the River of the Mountains, the continually flowing waters. From its high banks where they stood they could see food on the other side, a stand of ripened corn. Now, the Turkey, which shot off at the mouth, bragged he could get across to the corn first and the Turtle said the same. But the Wolf, pacing back and forth on the river bank, gave up right there. Then the Turkey ran back into the woods and gave a running start, cackling away and flew off, just grazing the water's surface. But halfway across the Great River, his heavy body pulled him down, and he gave out, falling into the water. Floundering around in the middle of the river, he managed to swim back to the shore where the Wolf and the Turtle sat watching him, laughing.

While the Turkey sat shivering, his feathers soaked to the skin, and the Wolf ran up and down the bank howling, the Turtle just slipped quietly into the deep river and walked across underwater on the bottom, rising on the far side to gorge himself with ripe corn.'

That is why," said Black Turtle with a smile, "the Turtle won the argument, and they decided that the Turtle was sure enough the best, the Turkey next, and the Wolf last."

Black Turtle, near the end of his story, drew hard on his pipe. Exhaling a cloud of smoke, he took another drag and shot out a row of perfect smoke rings, spiraling up above his grey head, chasing the cloud of tobacco smoke out the opening at the top of the lodge.

He concluded his tale.

"Mother Corn knew the *Unami* were the true Grandfathers of all the Indian peoples. *Pakoango,* the Crawler, the Great Turtle, which bears the world on its back, was our common ancestor, the first of all living beings. They were playmates, you know, the *Unami,* the *Minsi* and the *Unalachtigo;* who were like *Pullaeu,* that bird that does not chew, but gobbles his food down. And even these creatures in their playfulness and the Lenape likewise were the children of *Nanabush,* the Strong White One, Grandfather of all beings, Grandfather of men, who was on the Turtle Island. And the men were together on the Turtle, like to turtles. But *Nanabush* was the Grandfather of all beings, the Grandfather of men, the Grandfather of the Turtle."

Thus ended that day Black Turtle's tale of how the Turtle Clan came to be the best.

Mechkalanne's thoughts turned back to the path down which he trotted as he ran through the forest, eager to reach the village, to greet his adoptive parents, She Bear and Black Turtle. He knew that another tale awaited him from the fertile mind of the sachem.

*   *   *   *

The band of twelve pushed off in their dugout canoes, leaving Mechkalanne standing on the boulder at the edge of the *Mahicanituk*. They did not grip his hand in farewell. Possum Eater, made a gesture of contempt to Mechkalanne, their canoes, single file, darting out onto the endless expanse of the Great River. They disappeared into a cloud of rising fog, the canoes knifing through the still water. There was the muffled swish of each stroke as the strong-armed braves plunged their oars into the glassy mirror.

The flotilla soon arrived at the far shore, sliding like a water snake along the bank. They continued down river, masked by heavy, overhanging boughs of willow and cattail. Hidden from view from above, the braves caught glimpse of a meadow ahead, smoke rising lazily in the still morning air from the camp fires of a Wappinger Indian village standing at river's edge. They heard children's voices as they played quoits. Possum Eater and his followers drifted by, undetected by the Wappingers who, if they had spotted them, would have alerted the white squatters on the nearby patent of the approach of the war party. The dugouts slid on down river, its silence broken by the flight of a startled heron, its long, skinny legs submerged in the murky waters of a small stream at a point where it joined the continually flowing waters. The regal bird was fishing for small clams lying on the bottom at the creek's outlet. The cries of the children faded as Possum Eater led the band of marauders on down river.

The river meadows disappeared, surrendering to a cedar swamp, the river widening further. The twelve braves maneuvered their war canoes into a cove hidden from view until they were on top of it. There was the sharp smell of cedar and a worn footpath breaking out of the thicket, running off into the woods. The excited men leaped from their canoes, waist deep in the dark water, straining to pull their war crafts up under the protective mantle overhanging the river bank. The parting brush rustled, protesting their intrusion. The river current came to a halt here. The canoes would lie secure in the stagnant water, hidden from view until their return, within easy reach in case they needed to make a quick escape.

They pulled themselves, one at a time, up onto the soft, moss-covered river bank. Possum Eater signaled his men to remain still until he had scouted the neighboring woods. When he returned, he ordered them to prepare for the war party. They quickly shed their deer skin leggings and leather loincloths.

Possum Eater addressed them.

"We will prepare for battle here on the banks of the River of the Mountains since Black Turtle and the elders of the village have forbidden us to make such preparations back at our lodges."

The Delaware were at peace after many years on the warpath against the English, beside their brothers, the *Plantschemen*. During those dark years of war, Black Turtle had seen his village dwindle from 300 to fewer than 150; only 50 able braves remained.

The women of the village had come to the sachem, begging him for peace. Black Turtle heard their pleas, heeding them. The Great Spirit came to him in a dream in the form of Mother Bear. The she bear rose up on her black paws to signal the end of the war. The sachem awoke from his dream, called a council meeting, told his vision to the men and women of the tribe, throwing to the ground his war belt of black and purple wampum. The men followed Black Turtle's gesture, discarding their belts, except for Possum Eater and his thrill-seeking followers.

The brooding brave had muttered under his breath.

"There will come another day for scalp taking."

He had stalked off followed by his men. He would not be appeased.

And now that day had come. The marauders stood tall and naked on the river bank, their leader praying to the Great Spirit.

"*Nanabush,* guide us to the squatters' cabins, make our strong legs work swiftly, our war clubs find their mark as they search out trophies of blond hair."

The braves set about preparing their bodies for war, painting each other's copper skin, dark red. Their heads were shaved except for a small lock on the crown where they fixed a single white feather. Each man dressed quickly, feeling particularly handsome.

Possum Eater praised their appearance.

"It is a pity that our people cannot see us now. If so, there would be a war dance, and the women would be there to watch us and share in our joy."

Although they were not to sleep with their women since it was forbidden under punishment of death from the Great Spirit, they would ignore this warning, taking their pleasure with them before setting out on their foray. The darkness of night hiding this illicit pleasure, they would whisper their courage to their women, sighs rising from their lodges, sure signs of the joy their women would give them. Such a night would produce many good warriors to replace those who died on the raid, or who turned grey and wrinkled, according to the wishes of the Great Spirit. Times had changed among the Lenape since the days of their ancestors, old age descending quickly on their strong, young braves.

Possum Eater led his band through the spruce and cedar forest, up from the *Mahicanituk* into the highlands, each warrior carrying his provisions around his waist in a buckskin pouch. Shadows lengthened. Soon they breached the mountains, searching for a spot to spend the night. Sunset found them encamped in a clearing. They secured their weapons, covering them with deerskin. Their war clubs lay within arm's reach.

The band arose at sunrise, disappearing into the forest. As they trotted silently along the trail, Possum Eater called back to them.

"We will find the squatters' cabins and wait until dark to attack them while they are sleeping."

They ran across a level plain, gaining speed as it turned into a gentle slope, pointing them in the direction of the lowlands around Canopus Hollow. There was no sign of the white squatters and their cabins, their nearest settlement far to the north.

The band ran along the banks of Canopus Pond, then slipped back into the forest. Descending the trail, they glimpsed a clearing leading to the Tidd's corn patch, where Jacob and Esther were laboring, just beyond a hillock, hidden from view by the remaining stand of tattered corn stalks. The corn was taller than a grown man from abundant rainfall and warm, humid summer nights. The braves slipped closer to the Tidd cabin. The stockade fence came into view, and there were the voices of the three children, busy with their chores.

Possum Eater crept up to the stockade. Through the slots in the fence he caught a glimpse of Rebecca, Polly and Aaron working in the yard, his sharp eyes fixed on their red hair. He pictured Aaron's long, curly locks hanging from his war belt. He spotted Polly and then Rebecca, drawn to her thin, willowy form. He could not take his eyes off her. I will have her, he decided. His brain was fuzzy, his breath fetid from the firewater gulped down at their last stop. He had shared the bottle of whisky with his men, the drink sending images of glory racing through his mind.

"We will be rewarded when we return with such handsome trophies to our people on the *Lenapewihituk*."

The braves heeded his words.

They watched the children busy with their chores, and when Possum Eater was sure the three were alone, he decided that they did not need the cloak of darkness. He signaled the attack. The braves scaled the fence in an eye's blink. Sliding over the enclosure, they landed softly on the ground, their light moccasins making no sound. They were on top of the children in a flash, Possum Eater the first to reach Rebecca, bent over her bucket of apples. He pulled her soft body up to his bare chest. His dark red painted face, his shaved head, fetid breath and sweat-covered naked torso consumed her. He clasped his right hand over her mouth, opened wide in a futile attempt to scream. He wrapped his tattooed left arm, encircled from shoulder to wrist with the black coils of a water snake, around her narrow waist. He slung Rebecca over his shoulders, handing his prize to another brave who quickly tied leather thongs around her wrists and ankles, her long hair swinging wildly from side to side. Her bright blue eyes opened wide. She vomited. It had to be some hideous monster from the woods. It never dawned on her that it was a Lenape, a dreaded Delaware marauder.

Polly's captor treated her alike, but after seeing Possum Eater subdue her older sister, she knew that to resist her attacker was futile. She gave in to him without a struggle. Hanging halfway down the brave's back, she spotted Rebecca struggling frantically, her terror-stricken face bobbing between her captor's legs. Polly felt smothered by the brave's hand clasped hard over her face. The smell of sweat, whisky, and urine swept up her nose. She fainted.

Young Aaron was the last to be captured by the wild men as he ran for his father's gun. It was too late. Three of the youngest braves ran him down, descending on him in silence, their usual blood-curdling war whoops stifled for fear of alerting the Tidds, still working in their corn patch, within earshot of the cabin. The brave wrapped a rag about the youth's eyes and mouth. His long, gangly legs thrashing in the air, they dragged him up to a large rock standing at the top of the hill behind the cabin, at the foot of the stockade where it rose at its highest point. They doubled Aaron's tall, skinny body forward, brought their war clubs down hard across his skull, splitting it wide open. Red liquid spurted out, spraying the bodies of the three braves. Aaron's life force splashed across their hairless chests and faces, creating a mosaic of lighter red blotches on the dark red of their painted torsos. The lead brave dropped his war club, drawing his hunting knife from its sheath at his waist. Wielding the knife in his right hand, he grabbed Aaron's locks with his left, pulling them tight. In three quick strokes, each at a different angle, he deftly removed the scalp, then ripped off the top of the boy's head. Grey matter flew in all directions, sticking to the painted man, adding its color to the mosaic mix. The brave released Aaron, who fell back, chest up, onto the rock at the top of the hill, his opened skull revealing the grey labyrinth of the top of his brains, his bright, youthful face hidden beneath a sheet of blood. He uttered not a word.

＊　　　＊　　　＊　　　＊

Mechkalanne arrived back at the Lenape village, hurrying to the sachem's lodge. The old man, waiting for him at the entrance, gave him his hand, welcoming him.

"I am glad to see you, Mechkalanne. Your looks are familiar. I see gladness and joy on your face."

He motioned the young brave to follow him. Crouching down, Mechkalanne disappeared into the hut behind the sachem.

When he told Black Turtle of his decision not to follow Possum Eater and his gang, the sachem nodded in approval. The two men fell silent. They did not speak for a long time. Finally, the sachem invited Mechkalanne to share his pipe. The brave knew that Black Turtle had something important to tell him, and he heeded the old man's request. They made themselves comfortable, warming their hands over the dying camp fire, a sign of mutual respect. The sachem then took up his pipe, placed a wad of tobacco in its large bowl, puffed it joyfully, handing it to Mechkalanne. He drew a long drag on the pipe, eager for the old man to get on with one of his tales.

Black Turtle took the bundle of notched, red and black sticks from a pouch hanging from his belt. He fingered each stick lovingly, choosing a long one from the middle of the bundle. He hesitated for a moment, then began his tale.

"There was once a gang of twelve braves who were mean and scornful, who refused to be sociable with any tribe. They were always looking for trouble, refused to ever stay home in their village but wanted to go far away so that they could rob and kill people."

Black Turtle puffed on his pipe.

"So one day these twelve troublemakers started out to hunt down some squatters to kill and scalp them so that they could brag about their courage and skill as warriors. It was a trip which lasted several days, so they had to camp many times, but all their efforts failed, for there wasn't a single trace of any human beings. As they were foraging, they ran across a trail of some creature that ran on in a broad, straight line. They wondered what in the world it could be and finally decided that it had to be a turtle; but its tracks told them that the turtle was a big one, in fact, one as big as one of our lodges. The gang trailed the creature for a long time, and when they finally caught up with it, they discovered that it was indeed a very large turtle. They then climbed up on the turtle's back to examine it. And since they were a lazy lot, they decided that they would ride the turtle and save themselves a lot of hard work walking.

So once they were all on its back, the turtle started up. And the gang of twelve traveled on the turtle's back for several days. When they got to the Big Water, they could go no further. But the big turtle did not stop there but kept on going towards the sea. All that the men could see was water without end, so they decided that they should jump off as the turtle entered the water. But they found they couldn't get off because they were stuck to the turtle's back. One man managed to tumble off, and as he ran away, he looked back to see the eleven remaining braves' heads disappearing under the sea.

When this one brave who had escaped returned to his people and told them what had happened, they all gathered together to figure out how to get the remaining eleven men back because all the people were convinced that the braves were not dead because of the strange way they had disappeared riding on the turtle's back. The Lenape decided to turn to their cousins, the Shawnee, for advice. The Shawnee had a medicine man who told the Lenape that he knew a medicine and its song which they could use to make the turtle return with the eleven men. So the older Shawnee and Lenape accompanied the brave back to where he had seen his brothers disappear on the back of the giant turtle. So then the old men, Shawnee and Lenape alike, camped on the spot where the turtle and its riders had disappeared; and there they made their medicine.

The Shawnee made bowls of bark in which they placed their medicine. The old men all sat in a half circle facing the Big Water and began to chant, calling for the turtle to return with the eleven men. As they chanted their song, they heard the roar of some sea animal, and then a giant crayfish appeared.

Other sea creatures emerged from the sea, and as each animal crawled out of the water, a man would push it back saying, 'We don't want you. We want the turtle to come.'

Finally, a big snake with long horns on its head rose up out of the water. It was the longest snake in the world, and as it emerged from the sea, there were bolts of lightning and all different colors in the air. As the creature approached the men and their medicine, they came near the creature to examine him as he lay still in front of them. They discovered that he was the prettiest animal they had ever seen, all decorated with different colors about his head.

When the Lenape saw this many-colored scaly sea snake, they decided to remove some of the scales to make medicine and for good luck. Some took scales from his neck, some from other parts of his long body.

And by the way," Black Turtle added as an afterthought, "those scales are still with the Lenape people. Some would take one of those scales and place it in a split of wood which he would then place in a tree branch. Then when there was drought, they would pour water on it, and it would be taken up to the region above and then there would be plenty of rain, sure enough. These scales are still used for a token for good luck in killing deer, trapping fur, and so forth.

Well, when the Lenape got their scales they wanted, they told the snake they didn't want him and pushed him back into the water like they had done to all the other sea creatures. When the snake returned to the Big Water, the old men heard another roaring sound. It was so loud a sound that the people knew it had to be the great turtle. Besides, they had every other creature from the sea come to their medicine except the turtle. The water rose like a giant wave had descended on the shore, and then they saw the turtle rise from the sea with those eleven men still sitting on its back all alive and well.

All the chiefs gathered together and chose one old man who was the wisest sachem and then asked him, 'How shall we let this giant turtle know our wishes?'

He replied, 'We will use tobacco. The Great Spirit put tobacco here on earth for such a time as this—to use whenever our people want something from the animals.'

So he walked up to the turtle and said, 'We don't want you. We want our men back.'

When he finished speaking to the turtle, he took some tobacco and tied it around the turtle's neck and said, 'Here's some tobacco that I give you. You can take it back to the Big Water with you.'

After this gift of tobacco to the great turtle, the eleven men began to stir as if they had been in a dream and now had come back to their senses like they were before they were taken away. They noticed that it was daylight and that the sun was shining. They started to get off the turtle's back and to walk away but only after the tobacco was tied around the creature's neck. The turtle had returned their power to them.

The eleven men had been on the turtle's back for six moons, and when they got off his back, they told their people that where they had been, under the water, everything looked the same as on earth except there was no sun. They had seen many people there, the same as here, and there were animals under the water just like there were here on earth. The men explained that the turtle had taken them because he wanted the other animals to look up to him, that is, those that were under the water, because the turtle had other people there with him under the water. Then the twelve men and all their people went home. And to this day, the Lenape have the turtle medicine, a powerful one, and they still use it."

Black Turtle, satisfied with his tale of the turtle, with its powerful medicine and tobacco, picked up a stick lying on the ground and snapped it across his knee.

"*Nkax,* I break it off."

Mechkalanne stood up in respect for Black Turtle's wonderful story-telling powers. He took his hand and shook it, then left the sachem's lodge. As he returned to his own lodge, he thought of the warning by the elders that it was forbidden to tell such tales other than during the long, cold Delaware winters, for fear that all the crawling creatures that lived in the ground would hear the story and would then creep out of their holes to retaliate against Black Turtle for disobeying the edict. He decided that the old man's medicine was more powerful than that of any of those creatures.

✴   ✴   ✴   ✴

When Polly awoke, she was swinging back and forth upside down. Blood rushing to her brain, she saw stars, her hair brushing against the earth of the trail beneath her. Two muscular calves danced before her. Peering up between the pair of hard-working legs, she spotted Rebecca dangling like a rag doll down the back of Possum Eater, her curtain of hair shifting to the rhythm of her captor's strides. She swung her head back around. A young brave was running close at her heels. Hanging from his black war belt was the bloody scalp of Aaron, blood still dripping from the tips of his locks. The brave's eyes were ablaze with his new token of power.

She knew the scalp was Aaron's. She tried to scream, but in vain. She was waiting to die; she wanted to die. And then she slipped back into sweet, numbing oblivion. She welcomed it; she longed for it.

When she came to, she was murmuring her mother's favorite psalm.

"He avenges the blood of the innocent. He remembers the oppressed. Nor does he forget the cry of the poor. He raises me from the gates of death."

She could see Esther sitting at the kitchen table, her eyes shut tight, reciting the sacred words.

She moaned.

"Pity me, O Lord. See how I suffer at the hands of those who hate me. I shall tell of your saving power in Zion and praise you at the gates of its cities. The wicked shall return to the nether world together with all the nations that forget God. The needy shall not be forgotten. The hopes of the poor shall not perish. Arise, O Lord, do not tolerate man's impudence. Let the nations be judged before your presence. Set terror over the nations, O Lord. Let them know that they are but mortal men. Selah!"

Her head fell back in a swoon. She did not awake for a long time.

*   *   *   *

The band of twelve warriors with their three war prizes: Polly, Rebecca, and Aaron's locks, Possum Eater at the lead, loped through the woods back up the trail they had descended to reach the Tidd homestead. They were headed back west toward the Highlands bordering the *Mahicanituk*. They stopped only to relieve themselves and to take an occasional bite of the dried corn meal secured in the pouches slung around their necks. The meal, broken into small cake-like squares, gave them the energy they needed to make their getaway and to tolerate the added burden of two fully grown paleface women. Bound and gagged, they hung over the braves' shoulders, dangling down their backs, like two deer carcasses.

The warming rays of the late afternoon October sun struck the unconscious Polly's forehead, shadowed by a grey pall. The trail had opened up onto a meadow, covered with tall grass. Sharp nettles dug painfully into her bare neck and shoulders, jarring her back into the light of day.

She sized up their situation.

"Aaron, sweet Aaron has been murdered, scalped, and the're takin' us back to their camp, God only knows where...."

She pictured Jacob and Esther, returning from their corn patch to find them gone, and bloodied Aaron, or what was left of him, struck down by some hideous, awful thing.

Would she ever see her parents again?

A wild, painted face, grimacing mouth and shaved head with hair lock, a single white feather flopping back and forth filled her vision. Each time she twisted around to look up, she spotted her carrier's deer skin pouch bouncing about his thick neck, containing his personal tokens. Her imagination took over.

"I wonder what terrible potions that pouch contains. What horrors await us. Will they kill us? Will they rape us? Will they throw us down a mountain or into a river or a deep pit? Will they burn or bury us alive, stone us, or hang us? I wish they'd killed me with Aaron back at the cabin. But Aaron is with the Lord. And who'll look after Rebecca?"

Before her flashed Canopus Hollow, their cabin, the Dutch church on Sunday mornings, her walks in the swamp, and Sarah, the sheep dog. She had forgotten about Sarah.

Little did she know that the dog lay lifeless in a pool of blood, bludgeoned by a brave's war club when she had leaped at his throat to protect Aaron from his assailant.

Polly was fully awake now, waves of nausea flooding through her body.

"O Lord, hear the prayer I utter. Let my cry for help come to you. Do not hide your presence from me on the day when I am in trouble. Incline your ear to me and help me. Answer me speedily on the day I call."

She clung to the words of the psalm.

"For my days pass away like smoke. The Lord looks down from his holy height. He looks from the heavens upon the earth, to hear the groans of the prisoners, to free those who are doomed to death The length of the exile has weakened me. The long journey has shortened my days. I pray to God whose years are without end. Let me not die in the midst of my days."

"I'll get through this somehow—or maybe I'll die, and then that'll be the end of that."

Silently, the band moved single file into the pine forest leading to the Hudson Highlands. The sun sank into a purple haze enveloping the mountains lying before them. Late afternoon heat and hazy light dropped off, dark shadows descending on the little band snaking into the heavily wooded foothills. Night was fast approaching.

Soon they emerged from a grove of maple and pine, coming to a halt. Their captors flung them roughly to the ground. They were lying at the edge of a small clearing.

Their ankles and wrists bright red from the tightly bound deer leather thongs, they sat at the foot of a lone cedar tree, each struggling to wiggle her body in the direction of the other. Their wide eyes comforted each other.

The men were crouched in a small circle, their faces flushed with excitement.

Each brave took the deer skin pouch hanging from his neck, removing a small token from it. Holding it in the palm of his hand, he muttered a prayer of thanks to his *Manitowuk* who had brought him safely through the attack—to be sure he had not harmed in some way his guardian spirit and the spirit of the animal, his brother, which the token represented. In the pouches there were bear teeth, bits of turtle shells, clam shells, and wampum—colorful sea shells and beads. Such medicine would surely bring success to the end of their raid.

They produced a piece of smoked deer meat and another square of the ground corn meal, wolfed them down in silence, eyeing the whiteness of the girls' necks and their long red hair. They discussed their plans for Polly and Rebecca Tidd.

Each brave spoke in turn as the cool, crisp October night deepened. The chill of the night air called for a campfire, but they were far from the safety of their lodges, and a fire would draw attention. There were Wappinger villages close by, and the village of Fishkill lay just beyond the mountains rising above their camp to the west and north.

Possum Eater stood.

"The thin, red-haired paleface will be mine. I will take her as my woman when we return to our village."

The other men grunted their approval, grudgingly, envying the prize which belonged rightfully to their leader. They glanced at Polly, her eyes averting the piercing, dark ones of the twelve painted red men. They were sharing the last of Possum Eater's whisky, each man taking a final swig from the bottle. They laughed as they stood in a circle, Polly's terror-stricken face amusing them.

The young brave who had put an end to Aarons' short life stared at her, his eyes wandering across her body, exploring each curve, the whiteness of her neck and calves, and her shapely knees which her half-raised legs and disheveled dress exposed. She felt the fearsome warrior's eyes undressing her, and the terror was back, climbing out of her gut into the pit of her stomach, encircling her waist, up her spine—stopping to fondle each of her breasts, reaching her neck, wrapping its icy fingers around her firm flesh.

She looked up to see him holding his hands behind his bronze back. She saw nothing in his piercing eyes but a cruel desire.

Polly prayed, the shadows of the forest and mountains rising above them. Thirst consumed her. Suddenly, a hand gently brushed against her cheeks, and the gag which had covered her mouth for half a day fell away. A deer skin pouch was placed against her chin and a trickle of cool water blessed her parched lips. She gulped down the sweet water. It had never tasted so good. She heard Rebecca gulping down water in the darkness as well.

"Rebecca! Is that you? Are you all right?"

There was no response and the gag was quickly replaced.

Polly lay back against a tree in the pitch black, moonless night.

"Why, Lord, have you allowed this grief to strike us down?"

She recited to herself the 23rd Psalm as she tried to recline, supporting herself against the soft wood of the cedar tree.

"The Lord is my shepherd. I shall not want. He maketh me to lie down in green pastures. He leadeth me beside the still waters. He restoreth my soul …"

She fell into a fitful sleep.

Polly jerked awake as sharp pain filled her vagina. Something knifed into her, penetrating her. She found herself bent over a log, head down, her dress and petticoat rolled up over her head, her stout legs spread-eagled. The brave with the piercing, fiercely cruel eyes was hunched over her behind, bending her down beneath him. His breath came in short, hard fits against her neck, and she smelled the stench of his liquored breath. His hard phallus was tearing at her, hurting her. She was nauseated.

As the red skin moaned, his hard body collapsed on top of Polly. A flood of semen spotted with drops of blood ran out of her vagina, following the brave's wilting penis as he withdrew, falling back and away from his depository. Her bleeding hymen throbbed in pain. A reddish creme flowed down the red man's bare painted thigh, drops of it nestling in her bush.

"Mommy! Where is my mommy? My dear mommy? I want my mommy. Where has she gone?"

Only a day had passed since Polly had been dragged off the Tidd homestead. Esther Tidd's loving eyes, her rare but reassuring smile, swam before her as she drifted off—leaving her violated body behind, rising to a place where she was safe, where no one could reach her to hurt her any more. She looked down on her degradation, observing her nightmare pass before her.

"Becca told me there'd come a day when a beau'd come courtin', askin' for my hand in marriage, that we'd lie together, our private parts'd meet. But who knew I'd lose it all to a stinkin' savage who'd take my maidenhood. I feel such shame! I want to die! Dear God! With that demon on top of me, like a bull on a heifer, drivin' into me. I can taste his smelly breath and greasy, stinkin' body! I can feel his brown thin' tearin' and rippin' me so down there. Him gruntin' and moanin' like a ruttin' buck and me like a piece of meat, torn apart, and damned forever."

The war party awoke at dawn, removing the girls' muffles for another swig of water from the water pouch. The twelve braves, standing before their bound captives, removed their loincloths, peeing in front of the girls. They turned their faces away in disgust and embarrassment. Two new braves, delegated as bearers, stepped forward, seizing them by their waists, slinging them over their shoulders. They began the most difficult leg of their journey, the trek up and over the mountain pass crossing the Hudson Highlands to retrieve their canoes hidden under the brush at river's edge. Polly was numb, her lips swollen from the gag, her ankles and wrists throbbing from the digging leather thongs. Her vagina was still sore from the violation of the preceding night. She prayed that her nightmare would soon end, and when her eyes met Rebecca's, she glanced away to hide her shame and humiliation. The blood and semen stains on her dress betrayed her efforts to hide her violation from her sister's questioning eyes. Rebecca looked away.

At the end of the second day, Polly heard water lapping at a near shore. A soft, cool evening breeze brushed her forehead, and she smelled the fresh, flowing waters of the Hudson close by. She thought about the strength and endurance of her captors. Her father had told her how the Indians would carry a black bear, weighing more than twice a grown man, many miles through the forest to their camps. She heard the guttural sounds of the wolf dialect. The braves were excited upon reaching their dugout canoes. Their escape, undetected, was at hand.

The trip across the *Mahicanituk* began the final leg in the war party's trek back to the banks of the *Lenapewihituk* and their village. The braves placed Rebecca and Polly, still bound and gagged, in the bottom of two dugouts. Excited, they pictured the welcome awaiting them back at their village by the younger members of their clan.

Rebecca's face was pale and feverish. The bear grease her captors had smeared over themselves to ward off insects and from which their bodies glistened, enhancing their bronzeness, had rubbed off on her hair, now dull and stringy. With her bound hands, Polly motioned in the direction of her sister, but her captors ignored her alarm over Rebecca's condition. They plopped Polly roughly into the bottom of the dugout. She was ready to explode from fear, thirst, and hunger. Her stomach was complaining loudly.

"Poor Rebecca! And Aaron! What will become of us?"

She rocked her body back and forth.

The return trip back across Hudson's River was longer and more difficult than the journey to the Tidd cabin, the war party rowing upstream against the strong current with the added burden of two grown paleface women. The voices of the Wappinger people rose from their village as the crafts slipped silently by. The children were still at play, their voices rising from the river bank meadow as the flotilla coursed upstream in the gathering dusk of the *Mahicanituk*.

It was dark when they drew up along the far side of the Hudson not far from where they had left Mechkalanne standing on the boulder two suns earlier. They lifted their captives from the dugouts, dropping them onto the soft grass of the river bank. Polly and Rebecca lay stunned, their dresses in tatters.

A strange, new feeling invaded Polly as she looked up at Possum Eater's grim, proud face staring down at her. "He's examinin' me like a piece of meat." Up from her gut rose a loathing. "I wish all these red skinned savages dead with all my heart and soul. I wish they'd die, be wiped clean from the face of the earth and from my memory forever."

She had never wished death on anyone, but she wished this with all her might, that they would just disappear, along with her night of shame. Her violator stood a short distance up the bank next to one of the canoes, arms crossed, chest thrust forward, triumphant. He smiled at her. She looked away, fantasizing the death of this beast, a death as cruel as the one he had inflicted on her.

Possum Eater strode up to them, waving his fist.

"You no talk! You talk, you die!"

He motioned to two braves who quickly knelt down, removing the girls' gags and fetters. Unable to stand up, they rolled into each other's arms, clinging to each other.

"My darling Becca! What'll become of us?"

Rebecca turned away from her, her eyes burning with hatred. She spit out, hissing like a wounded serpent.

"I'd rather die than let them touch me!"

Polly looked down in her shame, reaching out to comfort her older sister.

"And Aaron!" Rebecca's voice trailed off.

"Our Aaron! Oh, dear Jesus!"

She lay back in Polly's arms. Tears flowed from Polly's eyes. Rebecca's were dry, a thin veil of hate dimming them. She sat staring far off in the distance.

The two girls pulled their aching bodies up from the soft, thick grass of the river bank, half-standing, propped against each other. Their ankles and wrists were swollen from the leather thongs which had dug unmercifully into their soft flesh. Polly's face was puffy from crying.

Rebecca and Polly Tidd spent the second night of their captivity huddled against one another in the chill air on the banks of the continuously flowing waters. Freed from their bonds, they lay against one another in a fetal position, gathering in each other's body warmth. The comfort they drew from one another softened their pain, hunger and their living nightmare.

The next morning they were jarred awake by two men poking their gun barrels into their backs.

"Stand!" Move!"

They lifted them to their feet, goading them with their weapons.

Polly turned to Rebecca.

"There's no sense hollerin' for help now. We are beyond earshot of the Wappinger village."

They ripped their torn dresses off at the knees to make the next leg of the forced march more tolerable. Their captors gave them each a piece of dry corn meal and smoked venison before resuming their journey.* Rebecca took a bite of the tasty corn cake offered to her and spit it defiantly into the face of Possum Eater, standing by her side.

"This is what I think of your rotten food!"

White specks of corn meal splattered across his dark red painted face. It twisted in rage. He grabbed his war club from his belt, raising it above her head, positioning it to bring down on the girl's skull.

"Kill me, you beast! Please kill me!"

He looked down at his wife-to-be, bringing his weapon to a halt, frozen in mid air. She looked up at him, her eyes cold. He held the weapon directly above her skull, his powerful arms trembling. The war club began its descent again to its mark, only to halt once more in mid-air. He checked his weapon, made a barely audible grunt and turned his back to the defiant Rebecca.

Striding away, he motioned to his men to follow him. They drove the girls forward with their gun butts like two heifer cows which had wandered off, just as Jacob Tidd chased back his livestock when they escaped the protection of his stockade. The party quickened its pace.

The trail, which led away from Hudson's River, was more visible than the forest path they had followed back from Canopus Hollow. It was beaten down by foraging bands of Lenape roaming this land extending from the banks of the Hudson to the shores of the Delaware—their ancient homeland—long since threatened by the invading Dutch and English settlers arriving from the south and east and the marauding *Mengwe* from the north.

"The white men are snakes!" Possum Eater had once declared.

"They came to our land as predicted long ago by our wise sachems. We welcomed them with extended arms as brothers, as is our custom. We shared the rich bounties of our land with them, and they sent their long knives soldiers to kill our strongest, our bravest men. They raped our women, brought their horrible smallpox with them which devoured our bodies and ate out our hearts, disfiguring our handsome faces."

Possum Eater's soul was filled with bitterness and a desire for revenge inherited from a hundred years of treachery and deceit committed against his people by the paleface, this against the Lenni Lenape, the original men, the Grandfathers of all the Algonquin peoples.

He had taken it upon himself to be the avenger for five generations of peace-loving Lenape who had suffered at the hands of the descendants of that paleface—the large blue-eyed, red-haired, bearded paleface that the grandfather of Possum Eater's grandfather had taken for *Wehixamukes*, the white-eyed man, the returning God-Man, sent to his people as promised to them in ancient times by the Great Spirit.

"But they wore masks, disguises, like the trickster spirits, the *Maunutoowuk*. Their hearts were black," concluded Possum Eater.

"They are truly like the great horned serpent which rose once out of the Big Water from the east to devour our people, as our Grandfathers warned us."

Thus spoke Possum Eater.

On the long journey back to the Delaware, Possum Eater halted near a giant oak tree. The warrior examined the tree's massive trunk, studying it carefully. There were small notches carved into the wood, the sap still oozing down the rough bark. The message had been etched on its trunk within a sun of their arrival. The shape and size of the tree markings told him that the glyphs were the work of one of his brothers, a Lenape.

The etchings announced the recent passage of a band of *Mengwe*—Iroquois— a scouting party guarding the southern boundaries of their territory. The markings also told that the party consisted of seventy-five braves marching toward the north, that they had attacked a small fort near Kingston, New York, that they had taken twenty scalps, all males. Several women, (the number was not indicated), had been taken prisoner, to be carried to their villages as slaves.

Possum Eater smiled in approval. He was happy that the *Mengwe* had passed this way ahead of them. Such a war party was forbidden by the peace agreement between the Lenape and their cousins, just as it had been forbidden by the elders of his village.

The Delaware were the "petticoated peacemakers, the petticoated women," the *Mengwe* had declared. Possum Eater had repeated these words in utter contempt for the white wampum belt of peace given by the *Mengwe* to the Lenapes' fathers and grandfathers. Their women had begged for peace as their numbers dwindled during the war with the English—when the Lenape had joined the French to drive out the paleface squatters who were taking their land to clear and plow—driving away their brothers, the bear, wolves, and deer.

The band of twelve, their human spoils in tow, pressed on through the forest, moving out of the watershed of the valley of the Hudson and into the Delaware. The terrain grew rougher, more rocky and hilly, the deep green of pine replacing the golds and reds of the broadleaf forest of the Hudson Valley. A boulder-strewn landscape led to the final range of mountains, separating them from their mother

Lenapewihituk. A narrow footpath broke over the mountains, leading the band down into the valley of the Delaware. Unlike the Hudson, the Delaware was narrower, the mountains through which it carved its valley rising more sharply from its floor. The path descended abruptly to a ledge.

Rounding a sharp cliff, they came out onto the ledge from which they could see the blue waters of the Delaware below. The river rose far up the valley, a narrow ribbon, losing itself in the purple October mist. Below them was a small Indian village nestled between a palisade and the swiftly flowing, crystal clear waters of the *Lenapewihituk*. There came into view thatched, oval-shaped lodges and longhouses, some a few feet across, others forty to sixty feet long. Scattered, narrow spirals of smoke rose from the Lenape village.

Polly was limping badly, her cotton dress once showered with bright yellow daisies, now faded and torn. She was talking to herself.

"Dear Lord, how much longer must this torment last?!"

Rebecca stared straight ahead. Polly cast her bloodshot eyes down toward the settlement, gulping back tears. A moan escaped from her throat, now blotchy with scratches and leather burns. She crumpled into a heap, her aching legs giving way. Rebecca broke free, racing ahead to catch her sister as she collapsed. A brave stepped in front of her, pushing her roughly back with one foot. She bit her lips as she watched Polly sink into unconsciousness.

----

*The dried corn was the staple of the hunting or marauding Lenape. Its kernels were crushed to form a nutritious meal or roasted in hot ashes and then pulverized. They would mix the dried corn cake with water or sugar before eating it. This *psindamocan* or *rassmanane,* sustained them during long hunting trips or war forays since it was the most nourishing of foods and would last throughout a journey of many days.

LENAPEWIHITUK

The returning warriors filed proudly down the sharp ravine to the narrow valley floor and into their village, their captive paleface women in tow. The main dwellings of the Lenape settlement came into view. They were long, bark-covered lodges or huts built in a haphazard fashion along the banks of the Delaware. There were no streets or central plaza as in an Anglo-European village. The bark huts were built in three basic styles. There were round ones with dome-shaped roofs with a large hole gaping in the middle for smoke to escape from cooking fires. There were oblong lodges—longhouses—with ridge poles attached to pitched or arched roofs. The huts had no windows, and entry was made through a single doorway half the height of a man, covered with animal skins through which they crouched to enter.

Polly came to as her captors entered the village. Dozens of young men, women and children rushed from all directions, the nearby woods and fields, the banks of the stream and from outcroppings of rock above the river. The small children were naked and barefoot. The older ones wore moccasins to protect their feet from the river bottom and the sharp rocks jutting from the palisades which they were scaling.

The women stood back, timid, but their interest in welcoming the returning braves overcame their shyness. They wore knee-length deer skin skirts; they were bare breasted. Their features were soft, their round faces framed by long black braids.

The older women wore their hair tied in a knot in the back to form a square club, topped off with a round mother-of-pearl button. Their coarse black hair shone in the sunlight from bear grease. Like the braves of Possom's war party, their bodies glistened from it. They wore bands of wampum beads around their foreheads.

The men wore loincloths of soft deer skin. These breechclouts were drawn between their legs, brought up in front, and folded, front and back, left to hang from their belts. Leggings of fringed buckskin had been removed, the sun too warm. Their deer skin moccasins were decorated with shells, beads and dyed porcupine quills. Their bodies were adorned with pendants, necklaces, earrings, arm bands, and ankle chains made from colorful little stones, animal teeth and claws.

These handsome people had small, dark eyes, prominent cheekbones with skin that ranged from a swarthy cafe au lait tint to near black. Their teeth were unusually white, in sharp contrast with their copper skin.

The men were beardless, their facial hair pulled out by the roots with a tweezers devised from a hinged mussel shell. Their faces were painted red, black and white. The women had painted their eyelashes and cheeks red. Some had round, red spots on each cheek, and on the rims of each of her ears. They wore tattoos on their upper and lower arms, legs, and chests—birds, snakes,--these creatures representing their *manitowuk*.

The older mens' hair hung shoulder length. The younger ones had shaved their heads with a sharp flint or plucked out their beards. They wore a cock's comb in the center, this scalp lock greased to stand erect. They had let it grow long enough to knot into two braids, one hanging forward, secured with a mother-of-pearl clasp, the other hanging to the back. Each brave's crest was topped off with a large feather.

The crowd of villagers separated to let the band and their captives pass. Possum Eater and his men pushed Polly and Rebecca roughly along into the center of the village. Children, adults, young and old appeared from all quarters of the village, closing into a curious throng around them. The women giggled at the sight of the two paleface girls in tatters, their hair hanging in strings. The adults acted like excited children drawn to an unusual event. Several called out to the sisters in their strange tongue.

One woman reached out and pinched Polly's behind as she passed close by. The others laughed in amusement. She screamed.

"Don't touch me!"

Another woman reached out to gently stroke her matted, dirty locks. They drew close, staring at Polly's full head of red, curly hair. They called out to her.

"Mockwasaka, Mockwasaka!"

The crowd, flea-bitten dogs running at their heels, barking sharply, trailed after the war party in the direction of a small creek bordered by sweat lodges. They passed a longhouse standing at the east side of the village, heading for a domed lodge at the far end. It stood at the foot of a protective wall of rock rising straight up. This was the lodge of Black Turtle and his woman. The entire village, Possum Eater and his war party at the helm, stood before the sachem's lodge waiting quietly for him to emerge.

When the animal flap lifted up, out of the dark opening, in a half-crouched position, came long, grey hair, followed by the thin body and weather beaten face of Black Turtle. His skin was dark—almost black. His face, however, had few wrinkles. His eyes were small and piercing; and they sparkled. They were the eyes of a man who had lived many winters and had seen much—ironic, playful—the eyes of a man who had come to accept how little he could do to control his fate or that of his people. Black Turtle was dressed in buckskin leggings and a loincloth, much like the younger bucks.

Behind him stood an old woman, her lighter skin more wrinkled, her small, round face, prominent cheek bones and large nose remarkably similar to Black Turtle's. She could have been his sister. It was She Bear, his companion of many winters. The old woman stood behind the sachem, about to address Possum Eater. She waited as the old man gathered his thoughts. He spoke in a soft tone, his dialect that of the Turtle Tribe, the *Unami,* although he was surrounded by *Munsi,* the hill people. He nodded, his long, salt and pepper hair swaying back and forth. He reached out to take Possum Eater's hand.

He greeted the young warrior.

"I am glad to see you. Your looks are familiar. Your face expresses gladness and joy. You have returned, Possum Eater, with your war trophies. Your sister, White Fawn's death is now avenged. You led the war party with courage and daring against our warnings. What do you want now from this old man?"

Possum Eater shoved Polly forward, pushing Rebecca, who tried to grab her sister's outstretched hand, back into the crowd. He spoke in harsh, guttural tones.

"I have brought you a daughter, sachem."

He turned away, his peace offering completed, his duty fulfilled, leading Rebecca roughly away as she cried out for her younger sister.

"Polly, help me!!"

Polly tried to break free to follow the retreating Possum Eater and her sister, but She Bear reached out and grabbed her, pulling her back. She placed her wrinkled arm around the girl's waist, urging her to come with her. Polly could hear

Rebecca's screams. She watched her disappear into the crowd as Possum Eater dragged her away. She sobbed as she submitted to She Bear, surrendering to her gentle but firm urgings to withdraw to the safety of the sachem's lodge.

She followed the old woman into the dwelling, an open fire smoldering in the center of the earthen floor. Along the walls of the hut stretched tree limbs erected in tiers, covered with animal skins. They were used for beds and seats. A pole extended across the ceiling of the lodge where smoke rose from the fire. From the pole the old couple's food and medicine were hanging. There were strings of corn-cobs braided and strung together by their husks, clumps of roots and dried pumpkin strips. There were medicinal herbs, red cedar boughs, sacred to the Lenape, and ceremonial tobacco. Pottery vessels and wooden utensils were stored under the tiered platform around the edge of the lodge.

She Bear motioned to Polly to sit down, and she obeyed her. The old woman took a soft cloth, wiping the girl's hot face, gently daubing at her puffy eyes. The cloth exuded a familiar aroma, the same one Polly had smelled rising from the waters of Canopus Pond. It had been treated with a sweet smelling ointment. The coolness of the cloth and the fragrance soothed her; and she lay her head back against She Bear's strong arms and fell into a deep sleep.

In a dream, Polly was floating on a placid stream, which ran through a warm, green glade, its banks filled with sweet smelling flowers. She ripped from her body what was left of her pretty flowered dress, now in shreds, and dove naked into the refreshing waters, the dirt and sweat peeling away in scales, like a serpent's skin. She let her body sink into the cleansing stream, her breasts buoyed up, two lilies bobbing on the water's surface; she lay submerged in the healing waters.

She awoke from her dream with a start. She was lying at the side of the lodge on a bed of soft animal fur. Her dress was gone, her body bathed and oiled. A light perfume rose from her skin. It felt good. Her aching body was whole again, its numbness gone. She felt the caress of raccoon fur against her thighs. She was naked from the waist up, her breasts exposed; she was dressed in a deer skin skirt. Her hair had been washed and parted, her tresses hanging on either side of her breasts. She reached up and touched the crown of her head. Her thick hair felt soft; it had been washed in rain water. Peering up from her couch of animal fur, she found the lodge empty.

The flap to the entrance lifted up, and She Bear entered quietly. Polly sat up; the old woman motioned her to lie down and rest. She spoke to her in the soft, melodious tones of Black Turtle. Taking her long arms and clasping them together, she formed a cradle, rocking it gently back and forth, pointing to Polly.

Polly sat up with a bolt.

"Rebecca! Where is Rebecca?!"

Black Turtle entered the lodge, the light of early morning and the rising sun following him in, striking Polly's forehead.

He raised his wrinkled fingers to his lips to hush her and grunted.

"Rebecca safe. No harm."

His broken English and his reassuring tone relieved her. She Bear pointed proudly to the transformed Polly for Black Turtle to see. Her cheeks had regained their glow.

Facing her squarely, Black Turtle looked gravely into her eyes.

"You new daughter. You stay here with *Lenni Lenape*. You be happy glad. She Bear, Black Turtle, mother, father."

She squinted at him, uncomprehending.

The faint voice she had heard back at the cabin during the raid whispered in her ear.

"It's useless to resist. Submit and survive!"

At least she knew that Rebecca was close by, and she needed her.

She nodded to the old chief. The sachem's woman smiled.

Polly, uncomfortable in her Indian clothes and in her nakedness, raised her arms, crossing them, failing to cover her bare breasts. The sachem and his woman laughed.

"All Lenape women dress thus so. You be happy glad with dress. Simple dress good. Free spirit to fly high."

He raised his skinny arms above his grizzled head, pointing to the heavens. Polly sat rigid, her arms still crossed. She Bear reached under one of the tiered platforms, pulling out a beaver fur. Shuffling up to her, she covered the girl's bare shoulders and breasts, like a shawl. Polly breathed a sigh of relief, her eyes scanning the lodge. Black Turtle was gone. She smiled gratefully at the old woman, her teeth chattering. Her pallor returned.

She Bear reached under the tier, retrieving a crudely carved wooden bucket, a stone kettle, and a heavy blanket. Placing the items one inside the other, she motioned to Polly to follow her. She crouched down, pulling the flap aside, slipping out of the lodge, Polly at her heels. Pulling her by the arm, she shuffled across the village, hurrying by naked children running in play, dogs yapping at their heels.

Young couples sat on felled logs in front of their lodges, deep in conversation. Older women sat in small groups, heavy, round, stone pots and pestles at their feet. They were dropping handfuls of dried corn into them, grounding the maize into small bits of corn meal. They waved, smiling at She Bear and her new ward as they passed by.

The village had returned to its normal routine after the excitement of the previous day. Few of the mature men were visible. They were preparing for one of their fall hunting trips which would take them away from the village for many suns. As the couple passed in front of each bark hut, a fire burned where the women were preparing various foods. There were pits shaped like small silos dug in the ground next to each fire. These storage bins, bark covered and lined with straw, held corn and beans for the cold months, soon to arrive.

Large, clay stew pots, supported by stone piles, stood in the middle of the fires. Pieces of meat—bear and venison, and fowl—partridge, woodcock, and squirrel, were being skewered on sticks. The women were holding the sticks over the glowing embers of the dying campfires. Other pieces of meat were roasting, buried in the hot coals.

Wooden bowls, stone knives and spoons made of clam shells were piled next to the pits, ready for a hungry villager to stop for a meal. The Lenape ate singly or in small groups, sharing their food with family members and neighbors alike. They chose to eat only when hunger bid them to do so. The savory odor of the game meats turning on the skewers rose into the air. Polly's stomach turned.

She Bear, the wooden bucket and stone kettle on one arm, Polly's hand grasping the other, led her across the village to the sweat lodges. Dome shaped, they lined a small creek dropping out of the towering palisade above the village in the thin ribbon of a waterfall. It gave off a cloud of fine mist, catching the first rays of the rising sun, producing a perfect rainbow, arching above the lodges. The narrow stream rushed down a rocky precipice, plunging beyond the sweat lodges into the waiting arms of the Delaware—Mother *Lenapewihituk*.

The earth and stone sweat lodges used by the women of the clan were small, unlike the larger one on the opposite side of the village reserved for the men. Each one was large enough to hold one person. It was constructed of twelve poles, representing the twelve levels of the Lenape heaven, leading to the dwelling of the Creator, the Great Spirit. Flexible saplings, cut in seven foot lengths, were bent over to form a circular, geometric sphere six feet across. Skins, mats, and blankets were laid over the outer framework.

The fire, located in the center, was fed by twelve hardwood logs. When Polly and She Bear arrived at the sweat lodge, its fire was burning brightly. The old woman removed a mat of hemp and bark from the wooden bucket she carried to form a pallet, motioning the girl to lie down. Polly obeyed. She Bear quickly disrobed the paleface girl. Covering her naked body with animal skins, she slid her and the pallet through the opening in the bottom of the sweat lodge, leaving her head exposed.

The fire's warmth eased Polly's shaking. The old woman began to chant in a deep monotone while she gathered some rocks—twelve medium sized stones. Polly dozed off.

After the fire had burned down to form a bed of coals, She Bear disappeared. She returned, armed with her bucket filled with rocks. She was also dragging a split oak branch several feet long. Placing the rocks carefully in the fire, the old woman took the empty bucket, and swinging it with remarkable ease over the nearby rushing stream, she drew a full bucket of water.

After the rocks were heated white hot, she dragged the heavy bucket to the sweat lodge, dumping its contents through the hole in the top onto the rocks. Hissing steam rolled up, filling the lodge, surrounding the body of the sleeping Polly Tidd. All of the implements of this ancient Lenape ritual were numbered in groups of twelve: the lodge, the poles, the fire logs and the steam rocks, representing the twelve levels of the Lenape heaven. For the *Lenni Lenape*, these objects with their powerful spirits—stone, fire, and water, possessed healing power.

She Bear chanted. She sat down before the opening from which Polly's head emerged, her brow and cheeks studded with beads of sweat. As the old woman chanted, she continued to fill the bucket to overflowing with the cold spring-fed stream water, dumping it onto the smoldering hot coals. In her song, she called the fire, "Our Grandfathers," and the water, "Our Mother," beckoning their spiritual force to aid in the cure of the suffering Polly Tidd.

As Polly sweated out the fever from the two day forced march through the wilderness, She Bear prepared a hot drink on a nearby lodge fire, using the small stone kettle she had brought with her. She took a wooden ladle and spooned the hot liquid into the girl's mouth, parched by fever. The potion sent her body sweating even more. It poured from her brow as the sharp odor of wild sage filled the air.

She Bear warmed her wrinkled hands over the spitting stones. She shuffled on her knees, bending over Polly's perspiring body, rubbing it in a circular motion. The soothing massage, the sweating induced by the heat of the fire, and the hot, wild sage potion were drawing out the poisons which had invaded her body. She was sound asleep when the old sweat doctor finished her treatment. Polly was cleansed and purified.

She Bear's strong fingers poked at Polly's shoulder. She motioned to her to withdraw from the cramped interior of the sweat lodge, pointing to the small stream where it gathered in a pool just before its final plunge into Mother Delaware below. Polly, the pain vanished from her young face, her body lithe and light, looked up quizzically. She Bear pulled her to the banks of the pool, motioning to her to jump in.

She pushed the dozing girl into the pool, ducking her head under the water. Polly bobbed up, her eyes wide, gasping for air. The icy blue water streamed from her mouth and nose. She Bear smiled as Polly floundered about the pool; catching her breath, she began to swim vigorously.

The old woman was waiting with a thick animal hide towel to rub down Polly's tingling body. As the couple walked back to the lodge, they passed a crier who was making the rounds of the old men's lodges, calling, "*Pimook, pimook*, go to sweat, go to sweat."

The old men, resembling Black Turtle, came out of their respective lodges one by one, each carrying a small kettle like the one She Bear had used in Polly's cure. Each kettle carried its own potion, its own medicine. The old woman greeted them as they passed, nodding to each other.

They passed a half dozen bark-covered long houses standing on the banks of the river. Polly scanned the lodges and the villagers gathered nearby, searching for a glimpse of Rebecca and her captor. They were nowhere to be seen.

Polly's bad memories were fading, the Tidd Homestead, her parents, her brother, and Rebecca, forgotten for the moment, as the wilderness and the Lenape, the people of the *Lenapewihituk*, opened their arms and their hearts to this stranger, this paleface girl—no longer a squatter's daughter, but the daughter of a chief, a sachem, and his woman—a couple venerated by their people.

*   *   *   *

After Possum Eater had presented Polly to Black Turtle and She Bear, he strode off into the crowd of villagers, pushing Rebecca roughly across the village to its outskirts on the banks of the Delaware. She stumbled along the path, followed by her captor, pursued by a crowd of curious women and children. She kept calling for Polly, but each time she cried out her sister's name, or tried to look back, he poked her with his gun butt. She quickened her pace, the brave marching her in the direction of the river.

The crowd of curious bystanders and children, their ever-present dogs barking at their heels, dwindled. One by one, they dropped away, losing interest in the brave and his war trophy, returning to the activities they had been pursuing before they stopped to watch the thin, willowy paleface woman with the red hair and the strange looking flowered dress. One woman, running close by next to Rebecca, reached out to touch the thin garment to feel the texture of the material—cotton—foreign to these people. The children stared in fascination at Rebecca's pale white neck and straight hair, hanging in greasy, matted tangles down to her exposed shoulders. Her beauty struck them in spite of her disheveled, dirty appearance.

Some of the women drew close to her as she stumbled by, her captor at her heels. Brushing their hands lightly across the garment, they eyed each other, voicing their pleasure at the feel of the cotton fabric. The faded gold and yellow flowers, their petals still sparkling in the sunlight, met with their approval.

One woman tried to tear off a piece of the bodice for a closer inspection. Feeling the tug of the curious woman's hand, Rebecca screamed, reaching down to grab the bottom of her dress. It tore open, the sodden, worn material of the skirt pulling apart. Finally, it ripped off, left hanging in the hands of the startled woman. The rest of the dress barely covered Rebecca's torso, her small, firm breasts, legs and behind exposed to the searching eyes of the villagers. She sobbed, holding her hands over her exposed breasts. The few remaining curiosity seekers stared at the paleface woman, the red-faced, wild-eyed Possum Eater close behind.

The crowd was gone, and Rebecca and Possum Eater were alone as they neared two small neighboring domed huts at river's edge. The couple came to a halt before the first lodge, vacant, its campfire extinguished. There was no storage bin in front of the hut next to the embers—no curl of smoke rising from inside.

Possum Eater stopped Rebecca short of the first dwelling, pointing with his gun barrel to the entrance.

She was startled. She shivered. Obeying the brave's gesture, she stooped down, pulling aside the animal skin, scooting on her knees into the darkened lodge. Possum Eater did not follow his captive into the lodge, but turned and strode away, his shoulders arched back, his barrel chest thrust forward. Striding over to the neighboring hut, he entered with ease, disappearing inside.

Rebecca sat in the darkness of the abandoned lodge, her breath coming in short fits. She rolled over on her side, laying her head down on the bare ground. She pulled her chilled, exposed legs up in a fetal position. She fell asleep, praying as she drifted off never to awaken.

Rebecca dreamed she had escaped her tormentors, wiggling free from her fetters, the deer skin thongs falling away from her throbbing wrists and ankles. She was running like a scared rabbit down a path in the dense woods. She smelled cedar and pine. Then she caught a glimpse of Possum Eater, his eyes filled with rage. He was leaning over the edge of a deep well, peering down at his reflection on the surface of the water below. Indian lore said that the image of the person one was to marry would appear to him there.

He gazed downwards, Rebecca's face appearing, her blue eyes glowing in the dark. They flashed their emptiness back up at him. Suddenly the image disappeared, and in its place lay an empty, plain box of a coffin. Rebecca opened her mouth, to scream. Nothing came out. She ran on through the pine woods, fleeing through the darkness of a moonless night. She spotted a light ahead at the edge of the forest. It grew brighter and brighter; she ran towards it.

She broke out of the maize into a clearing. Before her stood the Tidd farm, lying in a patch of sunlight, and in the distance she spotted her parents, Jacob and Esther, standing at the doorway of their cabin, motioning to her to hurry over to them. And there was Aaron, tall and skinny, a grin on his round, freckled face.

Recognizing Rebecca, he waved to her. She ran as fast as her aching feet could carry her in the direction of the stockade; but as she approached the fence, it grew taller, its pine poles thicker, more foreboding. She could hear her parents and Aaron calling her and Polly's name, but when she tried to answer, only a squawk rose from her tight throat and parched mouth. She heard the sounds of the *Minsi* dialect behind her in the woods.

She stood below the stockade rising even higher above her. She fell to the ground and cried. Tears came to her dry eyes, tears she had held back for so long—it seemed her entire life. They rolled down her thin, sallow cheeks. She lay sobbing in the dark at the foot of the stockade.

When Rebecca awoke from her dream, a thin beam of light was streaming through a small hole in the lodge, half way up its eastern flank. She wiped hot tears from her cheeks. They burned to her touch. Her eyes fixed on the little hole. Through it, she saw the morning star dimming. It was the break of day. She groaned. The homecoming was only a dream.

She sat up, and turning to the entrance way, spotted a pile of Indian clothes lying just inside. It wasn't there the night before. There were warm animal furs, deer skin skirts and leggings, two pair of deer hide moccasins, with multicolored beads and handsome dyed porcupine quills bordering the handiwork. Next to the pile of clothes, neatly stacked, was a leather pouch filled with dried venison steak, nuts, berries and corn meal cakes. A fresh water pouch lay next to the provisions. There was an ornamental head band and a small pile of wampum beads. The objects were nuptial gifts—gifts left by the tender hands of Possum Eater.

Rebecca prayed quietly as daylight stole through the holes of the shabby lodge. Suddenly, a peaceful calm flooded over her. She knelt, reciting a prayer of supplication Esther had taught her.

"Dear Lord Jesus," she whispered. "Be my refuge. Be my source of protection and sustenance. Sustain me and my sister, Polly, in this den of iniquity. Save my soul. Pluck me from this hell on earth. Hear my words. Amen."

The footsteps of Rebecca's suitor sounded outside the hut. The animal hide, pulled back, revealing Possum Eater standing at the entrance, his legs bare, the red paint washed away, their thick calves visible through the opening. She bit her lips and cleared her throat. She sat in silence, looking straight ahead in the soft, early morning light. She did not move. Nor did Possum Eater. His muscular legs loomed like two tall columns before the hut.

She continued to pray. The words came strong and clear now.

"Give me strength, dear Lord, to face my enemy."

The words of Polly's David came to her lips.

"O Lord, hear my prayer. Let my cry for help come to you. Do not hide your presence from me on the day I call. My heart is stricken and withered like grass because I have forgotten how to eat food. I am so worn out with groaning that my skin sticks to my bones. All day my enemies taunt me. I eat ashes like bread. What I drink is mingled with tears. He looks from the heavens upon the earth, to hear the groans of the prisoners, to free those who are doomed to death. The length of the exile has weakened me; the long journey has shortened my days. I pray to God whose years are without end. Let me not die in the midst of my days."

Rebecca's prayer came to an end; she turned and looked up. Possum Eater towered over her. He was naked except for his loin cloth, the red paint gone from his face and his long torso. His grim face was softer, less frightening than before. His high cheekbones stood out more prominently without the red paint. His beady eyes glowered down at her—cruel, pitiless. She knew what she had to do. Her jaw set, she lifted her bare foot, and slowly, deliberately, she pushed the pile of nuptial gifts towards him, the wampum and beads tumbling from the top of the pile to the dirt floor. A cornered, wild animal, she looked up at her captor, her eyes filled with scorn. Possum Eater's eyes were empty. Suddenly, rage filled the brave's eyes. His pent-up sexual energy and her rejection of him joined together lust, loathing, rage, and revenge.

He reached down to his loincloth, seized his tomahawk, raising it high over Rebecca, her head lowered once more in prayer. He brought it down with all the strength he could muster on the bowed head of his bride-to-be. There was a dull thud.

Her body fell forward from its kneeling position, blood gushing, spouting up, a bright red fountain in the center of the darkened lodge. He pulled his bloodied war club out from her shattered skull, gathered his gifts in his muscular arms and strode calmly out of the hut into the early morning light, brightening as Sun's rays broke over the rocky palisades rising above the village.

*   *   *   *

Polly awoke from a horrible nightmare. She was sweating profusely in the thick animal fur covering her bed on the lowest platform at the side of the lodge. She breathed a sigh of relief.

"It was only a dream, thank the Lord."

In the dream she heard Becca cry out her name. Her life was in danger. She was relieved, feeling Rebecca's presence in the lodge.

"I shall pray for Becca and keep prayin' for her as long as it takes for that savage to return her to my side where she belongs."

The cure in the sweat lodge under the old woman's expert hands had renewed her strength. She had faith that her sister and she would survive this ordeal and be reunited.

She thought out loud.

"The Lord has not brought us this far into the land of the Delaware to let us perish at the hands of those red devils."

She felt safe in the warm lodge of the old couple, sure somehow that Rebecca was also safe. She could finally relax. She let her head fall back into the cushioned raccoon fur wrapping her naked body, sleep soon overtaking her, and she drifted off. She did not awake until another sun rose over the land of the *Lenni Lenape*, grandfathers of all the Indian peoples of the East, their spiritual fathers from the earliest of times.

Polly awoke to the yapping of the village dogs with their little pointed ears and the laughter of the children running in play. It was early morning. A full sun had passed since she fell asleep in the sachem's lodge. As she stirred in her soft, safe nest, she heard the voices of Black Turtle and She Bear, the melodious sounds of the Turtle dialect, a pleasant contrast to the harsh, guttural words of the *Minsi* clan. The Wolf dialect reminded her of Possum Eater and his braves. She thought of Black Turtle's broken English, wondering where he had learned it. She remembered her mother describing how the Moravian missionaries had lived for years among the Indians, learning their language and customs, converting many of them to Christianity.

If she and her sister were threatened, she could turn to Black Turtle and She Bear. She was grateful to the old couple for taking her in. For the first time since she had been dragged off the Tidd homestead by the war party, she felt safe from Possum Eater. But she still wanted him dead. She whispered to herself, "I must pray for him and his soul as Mama would tell me to do so that I can rid him from my conscious thoughts and my life."

She returned to her prayers.

Black Turtle shuffled out of his lodge and into the early morning light, leaving She Bear to prepare Polly for her introduction to the people of the Delaware. The old woman placed in her arms a leather skirt and leggings. She had devised a makeshift halter to cover her breasts with ties secured in the back. The paleface girl, smiling timidly, looked up at the old woman, relieved. She Bear broke into a smile, which did not come easily to her passive face. Her face radiated warmth along with a certain sadness.

Polly wondered about She Bear's earlier life. Where were her children? Where did she come from? The Lenape children were close to their parents—even the fully grown ones—their lodges sitting next to their parents'. She had spotted them sitting and walking with their elders. She felt a little less homesick. It wasn't that different, after all, from her own family—at least, the family she once had. She wondered if she'd ever have that family back again. She shook the thought from her mind.

Polly slowly pulled on the skirt and the makeshift halter She Bear had fashioned for her. She felt strange wearing such odd garments. But she was glad her nakedness was covered. She dressed quickly, donning her new moccasins. When she was satisfied with the suit of beaver skin, she turned around in a quick circle so that She Bear could inspect her. She clapped her hands twice. Polly, embarrassed, was happy with the old woman's gesture.

The two of them crouched down, slipping out of the lodge into the golden light of late October. The sky was deep blue, the waters of Mother Delaware calling the children down to its banks for an autumn swim. They gathered on a sand bar, bare of the rocks scattered across the river bottom. Running naked through the water, they splashed each other, pitching a small ball, a *quoit*, back and forth. The older children dominated the match, this Lenape version of water polo. Their play time soon ended as the members of the clan turned to their daily tasks.

The women and children were harvesting the corn from the Lenape corn fields down river. The abundant harvest would sustain them until the fertile lands of the river bottom were exhausted, and then the clan would move on to another spot along the Delaware or further west, where they would burn the virgin pine and broadleaf forest to clear more land for their next corn field. The *Lenni Lenape* were a corn fed people.*

After their morning play, the children joined the women in shucking the corn, removing the kernels with a crude stone spoon. The corn lay in the sun to dry before being crushed into corn meal or hominy. Then they would add water and sugar to make corn meal cakes. These were consumed by the hunters, warriors, all the Lenape men who traveled great distances in search of game, mainly deer and bear, and to defend their territory from the wave of white squatters encroaching on their hunting grounds and from their enemies as well.

Polly and She Bear walked hand in hand across the village among the playing, working women and children. The couple was headed in the direction of the Big House standing at the far corner of the village, below the rocky palisades, on the opposite side of the village from the women's sweat lodges.

The Lenape Big House was reserved for council meetings and the yearly ceremonies held to celebrate the harvest of the corn—a time to remember their ancestors whom they venerated, a time of worship and thankfulness to the Great Spirit for bringing his chosen people safely to the banks of the Delaware from their ancestral home far to the west and north. The Big House ceremonies were fast approaching, and it was one of the duties of She Bear and two older women to clean the ceremonial building and prepare it for the twelve days of ritual dance and chants commemorating the harvest of the corn.

Polly and She Bear approached the Big House. Polly spotted a group of braves standing silently near the ceremonial house, in prayer and meditation. It was the first time she saw the young men of the village other than the renegades who were hanging around their women, still looking for praise for their escapade, and more trouble. The rest of the village men were preparing for the first of the fall hunts for meat for the coming winter. The hunting parties lasted many days, and the Lenape traveled great distances to the far corners of their hunting grounds, reserved by agreement with the *Mengwe*.

This hunt would be short-lived, but enough venison and bear meat would be taken to satisfy the needs of the clan during the feasts concluding the Big House celebration. The ceremonies, including stomp dancing, chanting, fasting and prayers, would last twelve days.

As Polly and her protector neared the group of braves, it struck her that the men were naked, their copper bodies studded with beads of sweat. She spotted a sweat lodge for the men, constructed like the small one she had occupied. The lodge was large enough to contain the dozen or so braves emerging from it.

Polly looked away so as not to see them naked, but as they quickened their pace to hurry by, she sneaked a quick peak back at the braves. One was standing close by, his arms crossed, his head erect. He was taller than the others by almost a head.

She couldn't take her eyes off his handsome face, square chin, chiseled chest and stomach. His small, dark eyes met her large, round blue ones. Her heart gave a bound. His eyes were not heartless and cold like Possum Eater's; rather they were soft like a fawn's and gentle. From these curious eyes gazing down at her flowed energy and intelligence. She gulped; her breath came up short. Her heart skipped another beat as she looked away, avoiding the naked brave's curious, friendly stare.

----

*Corn was prepared in a variety of ways by the Lenape. They roasted corn on the cob in the hot ashes of their hearth fires, or boiled it in water, with the husks intact. They knew the corn lost its goodness and sweetness if the husks were removed before cooking. Like many Indian peoples, they believed that unspoiled, natural foods, untainted by the hands of men, made a simpler, cleaner life before they were summoned to the land of the Great Spirit. Mother Corn was as sacred to them as the Great Hare, the Light of the Great Spirit, *Manitu* himself. The corn kernels were also used to make succotash—a mixture of corn and beans, or boiled to make hominy—a popular dish with the Lenape.

Polly stumbled along behind the old woman who was yanking her away from the naked men chanting a purification rite. Such a ceremony, the women were strictly forbidden to watch. But Polly could not erase from her mind the image of the handsome brave. King David returned to her fancy—David, the poet. She wondered if this was he—if such a thing could be—then, shook the thought away, catching up with She Bear, already standing at the entrance to the Big House.

The building was dark and empty, filled with dust. It resembled a white man's log cabin, built with heavy, bark-covered pine logs, its domed roof thatched with elm bark like that used to build the longhouses and smaller lodges. It was twenty-five feet wide by sixty feet long, with a door at each end facing east and west. They entered slowly, heavy oak doors complaining loudly. Polly looked around the Big House, awestruck. She recognized the layout of the lodge as a symbolic representation of Mother Earth. The four walls faced the four winds, with a central column connecting the "sky" above to the "earth" below.

On either side—to the east and west—of the oaken center post were two carved identical faces, each with a single, deeply indented eye socket running across its width. This sculpted effect extended in a convex curve across the top, interrupted by a broad-ridged aquiline nose, a large, square mouth dropping down to form a similarly shaped chin. She had never seen such sharp, angular features on a face before. The large, square mouth and extended chin stretched across the bottom of the carved, wooden face, topped off by thin, protruding lips curving down to a grimacing frown. Above the carved opening for the narrow lips, a wide fortrum extended across the width of the face, meeting the outside angles formed by the chin, mouth, eyes, and forehead. The entire face was symmetrical, oblong in height, with intersecting grooves on its broad, high forehead, creating the effect of pronounced frown lines, these lines filling a space as tall as the rest of the figure. She Bear pointed to the strange faces staring down at them.

M'Sing! she uttered.

It was the Masked Spirit, Gamekeeper in the Delaware theogony. Each of the carved faces was painted half black and half red, the frown wrinkles incised across the massive forehead. The face represented age and wisdom. She Bear pointed to the masks, signaling Polly to approach them.

"*Danus!*"

Polly did not understand. Then She Bear pointed to the frown wrinkles on the mask. Squinting to create her own scowl, she pointed again to the masks.

She repeated the gesture.

"*Danus.*"

Howahie, gunehunga, Danus!"

She turned toward Polly. Polly smiled, pointing to herself.

"*Danus?*"

The old woman smiled.

"*Danus.*"

She nodded her head in the direction of the four walls, and pointed successively to the north, east, south, and west.

"*Lowaniwi, Wapaniwi, Shawaniwi, Wunkeniwi.*"

Polly repeated them after her. They both smiled at the success of Polly's first words in the Lenape dialect.

The old woman pointed to herself.

"*Gauh, hase.*"

She clapped her hands together loudly as Polly, heartened, repeated her words.

Making a final inspection of the interior of the Big House, Polly spotted identical carvings on each of the six side posts and the four interior door posts. The glowering masks intrigued her. They reminded her of the face of Possum Eater. She shuddered at the thought, trying to focus on the ceremonial house. It was clear to her now. The Big House was the Lenape's depiction of the universe, with the dirt floor the Earth, and the four walls, the four quarters. Its vaulted ceiling was the sky where the Great Spirit, Manitou, the Lenape creator, reigned supreme.

Polly and She Bear swept the lodge clean, removing the ashes and burnt remains of two old holy fires which had burned on either side. They checked the gaping smoke holes in the vaulted roof, removing animal skins which had protected the interior from the elements. The holes were used to vent the smoke from the two fires which would burn during *Gamwing*. Making a final inspection to make sure the vents were clear and open, the two women left, returning to Black Turtle's lodge.

She Bear returned to the Big House many times that day accompanied by several women to prepare for the nightly ceremonies of *Gamwing*, which would begin within three suns. They would play the roles of the *ash-kah-suk*, the female attendants to the ceremony along with the male *ash-kah-suk*. To complete their task, the women freshly painted the carved faces black and white and prepared twelve prayer sticks, distributing piles of hay on which the participants in the various rituals would sit. Next to the doors, they placed large turkey wing feather spreads—to sweep the floor clean during the ceremonies, clearing a path to the Lenape heaven. They were also in charge of passing the twelve prayer sticks among the worshipers, placing fresh hay on the earthen floor after each ceremonial stomp dance, and keeping the two fires blazing.

Before returning to their lodges from their preparatory duties, the women brought a large earthen kettle, placing it outside the entrance to the Big House in which they prepared corn mush—sapan—to serve those in attendance. This hominy would bless the celebrants with spiritual strength. It was the duty of Black Turtle, as the leader of the *Unami* family, to invite the other Lenape clans living in the village, the *Minsi* and the *Unalachtigo*, to the *Gamwing*, or *Engomween*. It was his clan's obligation to prepare for this annual assembly of his people at harvest time.

The lodge was prepared. Black Turtle and She Bear, with Polly Tidd at their side, summoned the inhabitants of the village. Those men and women who chose to participate in the ceremony had to dress in their beaver skin robes and come to the Big House the following day to begin the twelve days and nights of commemoration of the creation of the world by the Great Spirit. During these twelve days, each of the male participants would have the chance to chant his dream, his personal vision.

The next evening the old couple painted their faces and dressed in their best attire, black and red robes. She Bear, presented Polly with her own robe, laying the garment before her daughter.

"For you, *Danus*, gift from sachem and old woman."

Polly, moved by the generosity of these people who had known her for such a short time, began to cry. Sensing the solemnity of the occasion and eager to show the sachem and his woman her respect for them and her gratitude, she quickly donned the special outfit. They left their lodge, walking solemnly towards the Big House as other members of the clan, their faces brightly painted, wearing their best robes and adorned with feathers and beads—moved singly and in pairs across the village towards the Big House.

As they approached the ceremonial lodge, Polly looked for Rebecca among the crowd of Indians; she was nowhere in sight. She turned to the sachem.

"Rebecca! Where is Rebecca?"

The old man's face grew grim. He was annoyed. She felt his discomfort at her question, so she did not pursue it.

A few steps beyond, the sachem turned to Polly.

"Rebecca good. No worry. Possum Eater treat good."

She felt his anxiety. As the trio descended to the ceremonial lodge, she said a short prayer to herself for Rebecca, a prayer that the dear Lord Jesus would care for her older sister, that Possum Eater would leave her unharmed. She would question She Bear about Rebecca another time.

As they approached the Big House, the old woman signaled to Polly to go with the sachem. She pointed to the ceremonial hall.

"*Danus*."

Polly nodded and followed the old man into the Big House. She Bear joined another woman and two men dressed in their ceremonial robes. Their job was to stand at each of the two entrances to the Big House and to direct the arriving guests to their places in the lodge.

From their assigned posts, the men would be the door keepers, and the women, armed with their turkey wing feather brooms, would sweep the floor clean after each of the dream vision orations and ritual dances. The men, dressed in their fancy robes, entered the lodge first, all sitting down in a tight semicircle, their legs crossed; the women sat behind the men, their faces solemn.

Black Turtle shuffled to the center of the lodge where the two sacred fires would blaze and where a pile of twelve sticks lay, carefully aligned in a circle, pointing to its center. The sachem produced two dry sticks from his long robe, rubbing them vigorously together until the straw beneath the firewood ignited. All faces stared at the floor, listening intently, as Black Turtle gathered his ritual implements around him, and sitting in the center of the circle of men, spoke in low, soft tones, his voice barely audible.

He chanted.

"We use these dry sticks to light the sacred fire that it may be pure."

The straw smoldered, then broke into flame as the sachem spoke to the participants.

"*Gamwing* requires a pure heart and mind of each of us, men and women alike. To properly carry out the required exercises throughout this period of twelve suns, we must practice abstinence from all pleasures of the flesh, for any brave to sleep with his woman is considered an unclean act. We must abstain from such pleasure throughout the *Keeshooh*, the twelve suns and moons of *Gamwing*."

"We are the *Lenee Lenaupa*, whom the Great Spirit, *Manitu*, the Great Spirit who came from *Woolit*, the Good, created. We believe in one Supreme Being—*Kaataunutoowit*, the Great Spirit, named for that which is great—*Khit*. This Being, our Source, who thought of us, created our World. He stayed on the Earth for some time admiring his creation.

Taking charge of the moral order, the order of the Good and all things connected with it, once he had perfected this order which he had created, he left it. Since his good presence was no longer needed, he left us *Manitowuk*, that is, all animals and all animated Nature, including plants, trees, all things which move and change in Nature and which possess his Light, his Energy: Vegetables, the Bear, Wolf, Turtle, Turkey, Sun, Moon, Trees, Wind and so forth—*Manitowuk*."

Looking up from his chant, his dark eyes circled around the hall.

"All the braves present have been prepared to meet their own *Manitowuk*, their guardian spirit. As young boys, they endured long fasting and extreme fatigue to excite their dream vision so that they might see with their own eyes their *Manitowuk* which had come to them in the form of a Turtle, Hawk, Eagle, our Grandfather Bear, a Wolf, the Wind and so forth. All those present who received this visitation have been directed by their *Manitowuk* concerning their future behavior and mannerisms.

Such a dream vision has great power, and in his private moments, the worshiper's life has been guided and controlled by his *Manitowuk*. All his prayers of thanks are songs he heard in his dream vision and which he now recounts at *Gamwing*. He repeats his dream often and at set times, thanking his *Manitowuk* whose wonderful intercession has brought about this man's good luck. His bad luck, he must attribute to his own bad conduct which has angered his guardian spirit."

Black Turtle nodded his head solemnly as he emphasized the importance of good deeds to the *Lenni Lenape*.

"These *Manitowuk* must answer to the Great Spirit who rules over them and guides them in their daily activities. Since he is the Chief Force operating behind them, we must direct our prayers of gratitude and supplication to Him—the Great Spirit and also to the Evil Spirits, the Tricksters, the *Maunutoowuk.*"

He paused, the lodge still. The silence frightened Polly. The lodge seemed empty. If the dark faces of the men and women were not illuminated by the blazing sacred fires, she would not have known that the lodge was filled to capacity with worshipers. Black Turtle, sensing her anxiety, lifted his bowed head and reached over, gently squeezing her hand.

He then spoke of the origin of *Gamwing* and the creation of their people.

"In the beginning there was only the Great Spirit, *Manito*. In the beginning there was nothing but water everywhere on the Earth. There was no land. There was only water and *Manito*; and the Great *Manito* brought up a Turtle from the deep. The water fell away from the Turtle's shell back, and a seed took root on the Turtle's back and grew into a small bush; this small bush grew into a tree. After the tree took firm root, it sent out a sprig, and this little bud grew into a man. A second sprout grew out of the Turtle's back which became woman.

From this couple the *Lenni Lenape* came forth. The Turtle, our Mother Earth, gave forth life, and it breathed in and out, thus creating the Tides. The twelve plates in the Earth's crust became our sacred number. The Great *Manito* gave the four corners of the Earth to our Grandfathers, also our Powerful *Manitowuk*, whom we call on for our protection, the guardians of our crops, our corn, our food, our sustenance: *Lowaniwi, Wasaniwi, Shawaniwi, Wunkeniwi*, their duty to care for, to tend to the four quarters of the Earth."

Polly, deep in thought, occasionally responding to the soft rhythms of Black Turtle's Unami dialect, recognized the Lenape words for the four directions. Their meaning dawned on her as the sachem's wrinkled, bare arms pointed in turn to each corner of the domed roof of the Big House.

"The Great *Manito* gave the duty of giving light to the Sun and to the Moon, *Kaso* and *Naboukekaso. Kaso* passed across the vault of the heavens from east to west, and at night *Kaso* went under the Earth. Our brothers, *Kaso* and *Naboukekaso*, our Elder Brothers, Manito gave them the duty of lighting the Earth, the whole Earth, *Pame, hau, com, meeke, cake*, by day and by night. Here were recognized their powers as Children of our Grandfathers—our Older Brothers."

Nearing the end of his introduction, Black Turtle concluded with the Lenape story of the origin of the *Gamwing* ceremony.

He fell into another period of silence, his eyes downcast. The participants did likewise, imitating the solemnity of the sachem. He then rose to his feet, producing a near black-shelled turtle rattle from his robe, giving the few small pebbles inside a vigorous shake.

At this signal, the worshipers stood. Black Turtle began to recount his vision. He repeated each phrase in a natural, ordinary tone of voice. After each utterance, the crowd, in a single voice, repeated it, word for word. He shook the turtle rattle from time to time, accompanied by three singers sitting off to his left, who also repeated each phrase or important word after each of his pauses. During this ritual, they beat a rolled, dry, deer skin drum in the shape of a tambourine, which they held in their laps. Slowly, softly they beat the drums with drumsticks, each with a hand grip carved in the form of a human head, identical to the twelve masked faces glaring down at them from the sides of the lodge.

From time to time during Black Turtle's story, some of the adults jumped to their feet and began to dance in movements of ten to twelve steps, stomping around the two fires on the hardened ground, moving counter clockwise around the lodge, all imitating the same strange dance step. The women formed a circle facing one direction, the men the opposite. While the men improvised arm movements, waving their arms like wings, sometimes acting as though they were charging, the women kept their knees slightly bent. Each time their heel or toe hit the ground, their knees responded by bending a little more, giving them a slight pumping motion as they moved along. Contrary to the men, the women kept their movements small, elbows at their sides, swinging their forearms left and right, up and down, raising their elbows level with their shoulders while rotating their wrists.

The men began their dance by stepping down on the ball of their right foot, bringing their left foot up to the right. They brought their right foot forward, always keeping their weight on the ball of each foot. Lifting their left knee, they bumped their right heel down on the ground, bringing their left foot down on the beat. They moved their right foot up next to their left, their left foot out again, heel up. Bumping their left heel down, they raised their right knee, coming back to their starting position.

The women's dance steps were more subdued, consisting mainly of twisting motions. With their toes pressed down firmly, they twisted on the balls of their feet, their heels off the ground. When they stopped twisting, their heels hit the ground on the beat. With their toes off the ground, they twisted on their heels.

They stopped twisting, while the balls of their feet hit the ground on the beat. With their heels off the ground, they twisted on the balls of their feet, their heels hitting the ground on the next beat.

The song they chanted came from deep within their throats. "Ha ne ye a na we ha ne ne ne ne he yo na ne ne ne ya na ya wa na le ha we ne ne he yo na ne ne ne ya na he yo wa na le ha we ne-----ha he ya no na na ya na he ho wa na lr ha we nr--------ya na yo wa na le ha we ne ya na yo wa na le ha we ne-------ya.

The beat of the drum, the stomp dance, Black Turtle's vision, chanted to the rhythm of the singers and dancers, mesmerized Polly. It cleared her mind, drawing her away from the sad, painful world from which she was slowly emerging, into the calm, transparent universe of the *Lenni Lenape,* a world which had created these healthful, robust, simple people. The soft, pleasant music, beat to the time of the four drum sticks with the human heads, left her hoping that she would some day experience a vision like Black Turtle's.

She forgot about her own vision of David, concluding that such dreams were reserved for the men. She wondered if the women had dream visions, and if they did, when would they get a chance to tell theirs? She would ask She Bear, sure she would have an answer for her.

Black Turtle finished his part of the ritual, concluding that the events recounted were foretold as he had related them and came to pass as was foretold. Each worshiper stood up, approaching the sachem, taking his hand and holding it for some time, after which they all returned to their places. He took out his clay pipe, placed a slug of tobacco in it and lit up, passing the pipe around for each man to smoke. As the ceremonial pipe passed around the Big House, those present kept the utmost silence and solemnity.

At this point in the ritual, She Bear and a companion entered the lodge with their turkey wing feather brooms, sweeping the aisles clear of the dust and straw raised by the chanting, stomping celebrants. The two women returned quickly to their posts outside the main entrance ways to the lodge.

Polly sat alone, absorbing the best she could the meaning of these scenes—the visions recounted by Black Turtle, and the communal chanting and stomp dances. During the periods of silence, she recited to herself the psalms of David. Some day, she thought, when I have mastered the *Unami* language, I'll share my vision of King David and the Bible with the Lenape.

On the second night of *Gamwing,* as the dream vision rituals continued, and Black Turtle's pipe passed from hand to hand, the sachem secretly pushed the turtle shell under his spindly legs to the man on his right, who repeated the gesture, slipping the rattle furtively to the man on his right. The turtle shell made its trip around the Big House in the same secretive manner until it reached the hands of a young brave, who, by giving the turtle shell a slight rattle, signaled his intention to speak his vision.

The brave sat quietly, head down, meditating, and then he rose to his feet, giving the rattle another shake. As he raised his bowed, shaved head, his braided scalp lock, hanging down his high forehead, swung to the side, revealing a youthful, angular face with prominent cheek bones.

Polly stared at the brave. It was Mechkalanne. His chiseled face and nose with the wide bridge reminded her of the masks scowling down at them from the center columns of the Big House—except that his face appeared radiant. His broad, high forehead was smooth and serene, not raised in the frown wrinkles of the masks.

Mechkalanne began to recount his vision.

"I am Mechkalanne, my *Manitowuk*, the sharp eyed bird who flies quickly across the land of the *Lenni Lenape*, followed by his fellow travelers, who claim his kill along with him. My *Manitowuk* are many: Loping White Wolf, the White Sturgeon, swimming in the deep of the *Mahicanituk*, my uncle, the Bald Eagle, who shares the sky with me, my little brother, the Bristling Porcupine, and our Grandfather, Black Bear, and, of course, crawling Turtle, the wise one, Grandfather of our grandfathers and grandmothers. My vision shines across the land of the Lenape. I come from the land of the *Minsi*—the Wolf people of the hills and mountains.

My dream vision begins when I was found in the ashes by my mother and father, She Bear and Black Turtle. Left to die by the paleface long knives, a small birdling, I was lifted up from out of the ashes by my mother and father, who carried me to the mountains from which I now fly high and wide. As I grew into a man, I loped with the Wolves, the *Minsi*, gobbled with the Turkey, the *Unalacht-igo*, crawled with the Turtle, the *Unami*'s and my spiritual home, which we carry within us. My dream vision stretches from the *Mahicanituk* to the *Lenapewihituk*, from the Big Water with its flowing ebb-tide in the East, to the Delaware in the West.

My memory stretches from the Land of the Turtles to the land of our ancestors and beyond. It carries us safely across the country of the Snake People. Like Bear Child of old, I was rescued from the clutches of the long knives. I still run free with the *Minsi*. As foretold to Black Turtle, I have brought honor to his lodge and to the lodges of the Lenape people."

Polly watched in awe as the crowd of Indians responded with strong emotions to Mechkalanne's story. His face was animated as he raised his long arms and broad hands, spreading them wide high above him, reaching up toward the domed roof of the Big House, to the heavens above, the dwelling place of *Manito*. The brave's sweet sounding voice, like Black Turtle's, rose from a low monotone to a higher pitch as he chanted his dream vision, his song rising from deep within his throat.

The celebrants leaped to their feet and began the stomp dance once more, in regular intervals of twelve steps each, this time with even greater enthusiasm. Polly felt the excitement in the Big House generated by the young brave's vision. He continued.

"All beings were friendly then when *Manito, Nanbush*, first thought of the Lenape, his people. All had cheerful knowledge, all were wise with much leisure, all thought only of cheerfulness and gladness. Only *Woolit*, the Good, existed— all beyond the Great Tidewater, at the first. Then we defeated the mighty Horned Snake with the help and guidance of *Nanbush*, the Mighty Horned Snake, who caused dissension and woe—great harm and injury to the Lenape, who destroyed their peace and caused them to hurt each other, brother against brother.

Then the Lenape fought this mighty Snake Person, who drove them from their peaceful lodges; they fought his destroyer, who brought the rushing waters and monsters to swallow us up; and then, *Nanbush*, Grandfather of us all, Grandfather of our grandfathers, Grandfather of all beings, came and saved us and carried us to Turtle Island, as was foretold; and it came to pass—*Nanbush, Nanbush*, the Grandfather of us all, of all Beings, of the Lenape, of the Turtle, of all creation. In that Northern Country, the Turtle Men of the Lenape were the strongest and the purest of heart. They were the hunters, the most noble, the best of the Lenape, the Turtle people.

And then the Turtle People left Turtle Island for Snake Island, and this their land burned, and it was torn asunder, and they left Snake Island, crossing over the frozen sea, the Great Tidal Sea; and they all came: the Eagle Clan, the Wolf Clan, the Beaver Clan.

They came from all over, the best men with their wives and daughters and faithful dogs; they came to the land of the Spruce Pines, and they came south to the Spruce Pine Land near the *Talligewi* people; and then they came to the East, to the Sunrise. *Wewoattan menatting tumaokan sakimanep.* 'The Wolf One,' wise in his counsel, was chief, and then Chitanwulit *sakimanep lowanuski, pallitonep*, the Strong Good One, was chief.

They fought against the Northerners—these my spiritual fathers, my Grand-fathers, they brought us to the *Talega* Land and helped us defeat the *Talligewis,* so that we could together come in peace to the sunrise, to the great and wide land, to the East land, a land without snakes, rich and pleasant, a land like our Turtle Island, the land of our ancestors—this new land, *Winachk Hacki,* Sassafras Land, a peaceful land, a land of plenty. And the Great Wonder Doer, *Manito,* did it all."

Mechkalanne's vision came to an end. He lowered his head in meditation. The whole company of celebrants jumped to their feet to perform their final stomp dance and chant in response to his vision.

After the hall grew quiet, the young brave took Black Turtle's pipe, and imi-tating his father, lit it, drew deeply, then passed it on around the lodge. At this point, the *ash-kah-suk* entered the lodge to sweep it clean as Mechkalanne handed the turtle rattle on. The other braves jumped to their feet, all eager to grasp his hand, to share this moment, to draw into their own visions, his vision.

When the first light of day broke through the smoke holes of the Big House, and shafts of light from the rising sun dropped over the palisades, streaking in through the open eastern doors of the Big House, the second night of worship of *Gamwing* had come and gone. During the third day, the men and women remained in the Big House in perfect silence. No word was uttered until sunset when the orations of the dream visions began again.

The ritual of the dream visions continued throughout the following nights of *Gamwing* until the break of each day when many braves followed the example of the sachem and his son. Black Turtle, She Bear, and Polly spent most of this time in the Big House while the male villagers seized the turtle rattle to signal their wish to share their own dreams.

During the twelve days of *Gamwing,* in the far corner of the lodge, sat a fear-some figure dressed in a bear skin, his head covered with a face mask. Its fang-filled mouth was often wide open, front paws rearing up. He would stand on his back paws, an enraged bear. The old bear man, the *mesinholikan,* occasion-ally rose from his post. With a long stick in his paw, he strode around the lodge, his terrifying mask causing alarm among the worshipers.

It was his duty to maintain order and to point out with his stick any man (or woman) who had been polluted by contact with the opposite sex during this twelve-day period of abstinence. When the bear man pointed at the "culprit," the person he deemed the guilty party, the *ash-kah-suk* would be called into the lodge to lead that person out, forbidden to return for the remaining days of *Gamwing.*

The *mesinholikan* was a foreboding sight, especially to those guilty of disobeying the rules of abstinence and personal conduct during the festival.

During the sixth night of *Gamwing*, as one of the elders was reciting his dream vision, the old man paused, struggling to find words to continue his story. Unable to proceed, and after a long pause, he stood up and announced that he found it impossible to continue his vision since it had been blocked by the improper conduct of one of the celebrants.

Aroused by the dream teller's complaint, the bear man stood, and with his frightful mask in place, began scrutinizing the entire crowd. He passed from celebrant to celebrant, many faces passive and stoic, some troubled and guilt-ridden. Finally, he raised his stick high in the air and pointed it at the dark face of a brave sitting in the far corner of the lodge, on the opposite side. It was Possum Eater.

The *mesinholikan*, in mock gravity, growled.

"This man is unclean! He has committed a terrible misdeed! Remove him from the lodge!"

Panic struck Possum Eater's face.

As the bear man called the *ash-kah-suk* to remove the renegade, his face twisted in an ugly rage. He slowly stood up, snarling, "This is false! This is a lie! You're an old fool!"

The enraged brave turned his back to the old man, stomping out of the Big House in defiance of the custom of allowing himself to be ejected from the lodge by the *ash-kah-suk*.

The crowd of worshipers gasped in one voice as the scene between the *Mesinholikan* and Possum Eater unfolded. The old man's mouth dropped open in disbelief. He was dumbfounded. The brave had desecrated the sanctity of *Gamwing*.

Polly sat paralyzed. Black Turtle recognized her agitation and reached out, gently placing his hand on her shoulder. The ritual recommenced.

With Possum Eater's exit from the rituals of *Gamwing*, the mood of the Big House grew somber. On the seventh night, to break the tension, Black Turtle rose from his seat and called out the names of six braves from among the worshipers, producing six strings of wampum, which he delivered to the *ash-kah-suk*. The braves were led out of the lodge. Crouching, they faced east. Howling like wolves, they repeated each wail in a prayerful tone, twelve times.

After receiving the strings of wampum from the four *ash-kah-suk*, they solemnly turned back to the lodge. The six braves then spread the grains of wampum throughout the lodge, this for the benefit of the *ash-kah-suk*. They had to retrieve them, using only one thumb and index finger while standing on one leg—to the amusement of all present.

As the twelve days of *Gamwing* drew to a close, Black Turtle urged his fellow Lenape to preserve in their utmost purity, the visions recited and the rites practiced during this time, and to meet the following *tachwoaks* at harvest. The sachem stressed that this was especially important since the numbers of their people were dwindling in face of the scourges brought to their land by the paleface.

He urged them to venerate in their daily prayers *Manito,* the Great Spirit, the author of their *Manitowuk,* the Lesser Spirits, in all their various forms and manifestations. When the sacred fires of *Gamwing* were extinguished, the hay removed, the floor of the Big House swept clean for the last time, Black Turtle, his woman, and his new daughter slowly walked in silence back to their lodge, their souls rejoicing, their spirits rekindled, their faces glowing with a new-found serenity.

Before falling asleep that night, Polly lay in the darkness of the sachem's lodge, reviewing the extraordinary events of the twelve days of *Gamwing.* She understood that *Nanbush* was the same creator, the Lord God Almighty that she had worshipped as a little girl.

Throughout the ceremonies, she had prayed to her Lord God and to his Son, Jesus Christ, that Rebecca would return safely to her side and that there would be a place for her older sister in the Turtle clan with Black Turtle and the matriarch, She Bear, in the land of the *Minsi* people. She whispered a prayer for Jacob and Esther Tidd and for her brother, Aaron's soul. The short time she had spent with the Lenape passed before her in the dim light of the lodge.

Polly, her past vanishing before her eyes, whispered her own dream vision to herself as she drifted off.

"He was of the tribe and house of David—*Depit, wetschithackep.*"

And then she was gone, replaced by the soundly sleeping *Danus,* daughter of She Bear and Black Turtle.

*　　　*　　　*　　　*

Small bands of Lenape left for the hunt after the Big House ceremonies, spreading out across their hunting territory. It would be a month before the *Tuk-ka-o*, led by Mechkalanne, would return to the Delaware village. Game was scarce and many Delaware clans had already pulled up their camps and begun the long journey across the mountains to the banks of the Susquehanna River following their brothers, the deer, black bear, otter and turkey. Even the black squirrels, abundant when the paleface first arrived, were rare with the intrusion of the white squatters into the Delaware hunting grounds. And the Lenape knew that the white man did not speak the language of their animal brothers and did not pray to their *Manitowuk* as they did. They were sure the animal spirits were angered by the ignorance of the white settlers. No longer were heard the necessary prayers of thankfulness and supplication to the beasts, which the Lenape had carried out from time immemorial. They had learned their lesson with the disappearance of Mother Corn; they understood the respect and veneration owed to all the spirits created by the Great *Nanabush*. The paleface did not understand this obligatory ritual, so the animals' numbers would continue to dwindle so long as these prayers were ignored. Each year now in late *Tachwoak*, following *Gamwing*, the Lenape hunters had to travel much further to find the deer herds. Especially rare was their grandfather bear, who needed greater expanses of forest to roam. The hunters tracked their brothers for many more suns, their return trip more difficult, burdened by the great distances they had to cover.

The hunters, with their leader, Mechkalanne, the most skillful among them, had spent many days in their sweat lodges, preparing for the hardships of the long hunting trips and to appease the *Manitowuk* of their brother animals. They would not return until the first snows fell along the upper reaches of the Delaware. As head of the hunting party, Mechkalanne urged the younger men, especially the lazy ones, to begin the hunt early every morning, directing them where to set up their hunting camps. Respected as closest in kinship to their animal brothers, he would execute the first kill.

Before the hunters had left their lodges, they built a fire. They tossed in a wad of tobacco to appease each man's *Manitowuk*, and the spirits of the animals they were pursuing. They set off in different directions, armed with bow and arrow, spears, as well as rifles and metal traps traded to them by the paleface. They would kill as much game as possible and as quickly as possible. Their clan's survival depended on it.

The first day, Mechkalanne ate nothing, preferring to begin the hunt on an empty stomach. Black Turtle had reminded him that hunger made the hunter work harder for the first kill, recalling the urgency of the hunt and its purpose— to keep their stomachs full throughout the long Delaware winter when they were snowbound and when many of their animal brothers were deep in winter sleep. A full belly made the hunter lazy and careless since he would be thinking of his village and his people, not the hunt. Mechkalanne hunted until darkness prevented him from spotting his prey—his stomach growling and whining all the time.

As twilight fell, his prayers were answered. Refusing to carry a gun, the paleface's weapon used against his people and his brother, the white-tailed deer, he brought down a stag with one arrow from his bow. Black Turtle had taught him the traditional Lenape hunting techniques, using their ancient weapons. Mech's arrowhead point, chipped from white quartz and razor-sharp, sped to its mark, the buck's jugular. It sank into the creature's neck, slicing in half the critical vein

The stag, with its towering rack, crashed to the forest floor, its hooves buckling out from under it. He dragged the dead animal back to his camp, spread apart its stiffening legs, placing his hunting knife at the proper spot to dress out the deer. He slit open the carcass, starting at the white flag of a tail, ending at the stag's chest. The thick hair, wiry and coarse, parted, the hide splitting open. Thick, coagulating blood oozed out, followed by billows of steaming, cream-to-pink viscera, rolling out of the gut cavity onto the leaf-covered forest floor. The entrails made a sucking sound, the sharp odor of fresh blood sweeping up from the dead beast.

Mech and his companions lit a fire for a feast of venison steak. As a token of gratitude to their *Manitowuk* and that of the deer, he took a pinch of *glicanican*, Indian ceremonial tobacco, from the pouch hanging about his neck. He pitched it into the flames, thanking the spirits accompanying him on the hunt for driving the stag his way in the forest. It was a token of his thankfulness for the good luck with which the *Manitowuk* favored them on the first day of the hunt. He cut off the best piece of venison steak from the animal's flank and roasted it on the hot ashes of the fire, inviting his friend, White Beaver, famished, took the piece of meat, wolfing it down.

While he devoured the deer meat, his teacher explained to him the purpose of this sacrifice. Mech then directed him to take the remaining venison out beyond the camp fire into the woods to finish it. He was then to return to the camp to thank his own *Manitowuk* for its favor and their good luck, praying that it might continue. This ritual would also appease any spirits not in favor of their hunting success.

The next morning's bright dawn found Mechkalanne sitting beside a small stream. Next to him lay the hulk of a black bear, one of his arrows jutting from the creature's huge neck. Like his brother deer, the bear's jugular vein had been severed. The grandfather's chest glistened with fresh blood, its shining black hairs raised in a garden of bloodied tufts. He sat beside the motionless animal, gazing sadly at it.

Staring into the creature's lifeless eyes, he prayed.

"Thank you friend that you did not make me rise this morning and walk about your land in vain. You have found me and have taken mercy upon me that I may inherit your power and skill in getting easily with your great bear paws the trout that you catch from this stream."

He then took hold of the animal's paw, continuing.

"Now I will press my hand against your paw, my friend, you who have come to have mercy upon me and my hunt."

He raise the beer paws in his two hands.

"Now my friend, we press our working hands together so that you may give over to me your power of fishing and gathering, of getting everything easily with your hands, friend."

Mechkalanne had appeased the *Manitowuk* of the bear. He drew his knife, and his propitiation complete, began to skin out the beast.

That night, as he prepared to sleep, Mechkalanne's thoughts turned to his people and the intriguing Polly Tidd. When he spotted her that day while standing with his brothers outside the sweat lodge, his own reaction to the paleface girl surprised him.

His heart had always been set on a Lenape girl, *Wapsu Amimi*, White Dove. Her parents had promised her to him when he had barely finished the period of fasting and self-denial, announcing his entry into manhood. The next winter she took sick and smallpox quickly ended her short life before he had gotten to know her.

After the death of White Dove, Black Turtle summoned Mechkalanne to his lodge and assured the disgruntled young brave that his future wife would come to him in a dream, and he would recognize her by her eyes into which he would peer to behold her pure spirit.

When his and Polly's eyes met that day at the sweat lodge, Black Turtle's words flashed through the brave's quick mind. Her eyes were like sea water, thought Mechkalanne, as he pursued his brothers and Grandfather through the forest, like the sea water from which Turtle Island had risen.

.He recalled Black Turtle's story of how the Great Manito had created the White Man from the froth churned up by the giant waves formed by Turtle Island emerging from the sea. He would turn to his dreams for direction and guidance in this matter. He fell asleep, relieved.

Polly sat up in the sachem's lodge, the image of Mechkalanne dancing before her eyes as a dream faded away.

*   *   *   *

Te-quaw-ko's days were waning, and the hunting party had not returned. While the hunters were gone, each clan member, from the youngest to the oldest, had an assigned task, preparing for the long Delaware winter, *Lo-wun*. This required the efforts of the entire village. In the land of the *Minsi*, the people of the upper Delaware valley, the stony people, the people of the rock-strewn plains and hills, and in the lands to the north and to the west, where the *Mengwe* ruled, the winters were longer and colder than in the land of the *Unami*, to the south along the river, or in the land of the Turkey Clan, the *Unalachtigo*, who dwelled further south and east near the Great Water. The *Minsi*, like their brother, the Wolf, knew that they had to range far from their lodges to secure the meat and skins needed to survive the severe winters.

Polly worked at the side of She Bear, grinding corn meal and preparing the smokehouse and curing sheds to receive the meat from the hunt. The bear meat and venison would be salted or smoked and the hides and furs preserved for winter robes, parkas and blankets.

While Polly's grasp of the *Unami* dialect grew, she questioned She Bear about her sister. The old woman knew nothing about Rebecca's whereabouts, but she promised she would seek out Possum Eater and question him and the other members of their clan. Polly's fear that Rebecca had been killed by Possum Eater grew as the days passed. Her heart sank at the thought that her sister, if not dead, had been taken to another village and that they would never see each other again.

One morning, Black Turtle awoke her, and placing his hands gently on her shoulders, he spoke to her in his broken English.

"*Danus*, Rebecca gone from village. Possum Eater gone from village."

"My poor Rebecca. Whatever has become of you?"

She sank into the old man's arms. He held her.

"*Danus, Danus!*"

Two more weeks passed, and the hunters were yet to return. If the weather turned bad, or if they were unsuccessful in their hunt, the Lenape retreated to caves near the banks of the Delaware, remaining there, praying, until the weather improved or until the luck of the hunt changed in their favor. Meanwhile, Polly occupied herself working at She Bear's side. She continued to learn the *Unami* dialect, her sharp ear picking up the language, her gifted tongue imitating its soft sounds.

One morning, She Bear beckoned Polly to her side and announced that from that moment on, she would call her Mockwasaka, Red-haired Woman. Polly swelled with pride at the sound of her new name which fit her perfectly, she thought. She had heard the name called out to her by the Indians many times since the first day of her arrival in their village. They were taken with her carrot-red hair. The name struck her fancy. She liked the ring of it. It had strength and character.

She repeated her new name in Delaware.

"Mockwasaka, Mockwasaka. I like it! Thank you, mother! My mother! *Nga-hase, nain-guk!*"

She embraced She Bear.

She Bear taught Mockwasaka many things during her first months among the Lenape people: to prepare a potage by boiling pounded meat, mixing it with dried beans, chestnuts and pumpkin. She mixed this corn potage with hickory nuts to add to its flavor. She taught her to cook dishes from squash, pumpkin, and beans. She told her that the less water she used to cook the vegetables, the tastier, stewed in their own juices. She Bear covered up the stewing pots with large leaves she had gathered at harvest—from pumpkin vines or from the outer leaves of harvested cabbages. She made cranberry and crabapple preserves, Mockwasaka's favorite, sweetened with molasses or maple sugar.

The village took on a somber look. And then snow fell, the Lenape awakening to the first hard freeze of winter. The small streams entering the Delaware were covered with a thin sheet of ice. Steam rose from the warmer water of the river, lifting up and encircling the tall spruce trees standing on the far banks of this, the swiftly flowing water. The frost-covered pines glittered in the dim morning sunshine. The frozen crystals covered the palisades, towering above the village in a sparkling mantle, transforming the river valley and the encampment.

One cold morning, Mockwasaka and the old couple woke to the yapping of dogs and the excited voices of villagers. Mechkalanne and his hunting party had returned. The braves stood in the center of the settlement, their strong backs loaded down with wild fowl—geese, ducks and partridge. Others were dragging or carrying on their backs the stilled hulks of black bear and deer, their dark brown hides topped by large sets of antlers, their tongues sticking out crazily from the sides of their mouths, their soft brown eyes glazed over.

The older women surrounded the returning hunters. They were eyeing the black fur of their grandfather bear, picturing the warm winter robes the animals' sacrifice would give them during the cold winter days and the long winter nights, fast approaching. They would be safe and warm in their lodges where they would spend most of the long winter, the opposite of the warm weather months when they were rarely found in their huts except at night when it was time to sleep.

Mockwasaka, her parents at her side, hurried out of Black Turtle's lodge to greet the hunters. Mechkalanne stood proudly next to a pile of dead animals with fur, horns, paws, and hooves, jutting out from the pile. The braves were wearing buckskin vests, their bare legs covered with warm leggings. Soon the entire clan surrounded the hunters and their kill. Their task completed, that of the old men, women and children now began. The animals were already dressed out; the hides would now be removed, the meat cured or smoked, and the women would busy themselves, turning the skins and furs into robes, blankets and buckskin skirts, vests, and leggings.

Mockwasaka and Mechkalanne looked for each other in the milling, excited crowd. When the hunter spotted her red hair and Indian dress with the makeshift halter, he smiled. Her eyes were glowing with renewed health. As he approached her, she looked down. His searching eyes met hers. That new feeling stirred within her—the one she felt the day she first spotted him.

He strode up to her and his adopted parents. His large, smooth hand took the old man's and woman's in turn, softly gripping them.

"I am glad to meet you and find you in good health and that your faces are full of joy and peace after *Gamwing*."

The old couple repeated his words, accepting his greetings.

He turned to Mockwasaka.

"Paleface woman make pretty squaw. Eyes as blue as sea water. Hair as red as sly fox. Mechkalanne happy glad to see sister Polly safe in my mother and father's lodge."

She Bear interrupted him.

"Polly now Mockwasaka."

She smiled shyly.

"Thank you, *Gahowes*. Thank you, *Noch*. Thank you Mechkalanne."

The brave took her hand, his long fingers dwarfing hers. Imitating her new parents, she bowed slightly to the returning brave, her face flushed. Sensing her agitation, he stepped back. She Bear took her by the arm and retreated to their lodge, leaving Mechkalanne and his followers to receive the welcoming villagers. Each of them spoke of their joy with the success of the hunt and their admiration for his and his brothers' skills.

Early one morning, a few days after the hunting party's return, Mechkalanne stood at the entrance to Black Turtle's lodge, his head bowed, the single white feather drooping down his broad forehead. Behind him, lying on a pallet in a thin layer of snow was Rebecca's frozen, decomposed body, its skeletal remains outlined, wrapped in a brightly colored blanket.

He had dragged her remains from behind the falls plunging off the palisades above the village and down their rocky face at the point where the stream emerged at the women's sweat lodges. He had stumbled by accident onto the corpse's resting place. The veil of water had been Rebecca's shroud since Possum Eater had dumped her body there many weeks earlier. Frozen strands of red hair, like pieces of straw covered with icy beads, stuck out from the end of the blanket.

Mockwaska emerged from the lodge at her parents' beckoning. She stared at the twisted figure lying behind Mechkalanne. She scrutinized his grim face staring at the ground. Suddenly, she recognized the mutilated corpse of Rebecca. She stared in disbelief, and then she moaned—as if the wind had been knocked out of her—and fell backwards into the waiting arms of She Bear. Her long wait was over. Rebecca had come home. An eerie wail rose high up to the towering palisades—bouncing off their rocky facade—echoing back and forth across the vast expanse of the *Lenapewihituk*.

The following day, four villagers arrived at the sachem's lodge to retrieve the remains of Rebecca Tidd. Her relationship to the sachem's family assured her a proper Indian burial and the respect, dignity and ceremony attending it. Rebecca was laid to rest the same day.

Two men, with the help of two women, washed and dressed the girl's remains in an elaborate beaver skin dress. They prepared a simple pine wood coffin in which they placed Rebecca, bearing her solemnly to the grave site not far from the waterfall where Mechkalanne had discovered her. The little clan walked slowly before the coffin and its bearers. The villagers filed behind.

When they arrived at the grave site, they found a freshly dug open grave three feet deep lined with bark which the men used to cover the coffin after lowering it into the partially frozen ground. Mechkalanne spoke softly to the coffin bearers, expressing his thanks to them for himself, his family, and his adopted sister, Mockwasaka.

Mock, numb from grief, stared at the throng, barely conscious of their concern, that they shared her sorrow. Before the burial party left the grave, the hole was refilled with the dark, rich soil of *Lenapewihituk*, the Delaware River bottom, dirt blanched with the first crystals of winter's frost. Mockwasaka knelt before her sister's grave, praying silently. The others bowed their heads.

During the days following the burial, Mechkalanne and the old couple accompanied Mockwasaka to the grave at sunrise and at sunset. The Delaware winter had turned bitter cold, but the four sat huddled together, wrapped in their heavy bear skin furs, their body heat warming each other. They sat on their hams, upon the grave, in silence, until late evening, their heads bowed, their eyes downcast.

The daily visits to Rebecca's grave comforted Mockwasaka. A bitter north wind howled down the valley of the Delaware, the river partially frozen, the winter blast shrieking through the giant spruce trees across the river and along the towering cliffs. The Wind itself had joined the small clan in its grief. Mockwasaka did not know of the Lenape custom of keeping company with the soul of the departed one in case it had not yet left for the land of the spirits.

During her mourning period, the villagers refrained from their usual games and amusements out of respect for their sachem's adopted daughter and her dead sister. They removed their adornments, their feathers and beads of which the Lenape are so fond, including the women's mother-of-pearl clasps, letting their long, jet-black hair hang loose about their necks. Mock felt comfort knowing that Rebecca lay close to the family's lodge—that she could visit and care for her grave and go to pray there with her often. From this thought she drew solace.

Before the clan left Rebecca's grave for the last time, several villagers arrived, presenting Mockwasaka and her family with meat from the fall hunt, and fruits and vegetables gathered from the harvest. They then gathered with the mourners for a final feast near Rebecca's grave. One young woman was invited to sit next to Mockwasaka and Mechkalanne and to eat that portion of the meal which would have been allotted to the departed Rebecca. The group, flanked by the sachem's family, crouched, eating in silence.

And when the feast was over, the invited guest stood to address the spirit of the departed Rebecca Tidd, telling her of the extreme regret of not only her family whom she had left behind, but of that of all the clan, who never came to know her. The young woman continued her prayer, begging Rebecca's spirit to rest in peace, to be glad with her new-found life, and imploring her not to return to take away with her any of her remaining family members. The woman spoke to Rebecca's spirit as to a sister. She spoke the words Mockwasaka could not speak.

"Behold, oh my sister. *Nanabush,* the Great Spirit, has taken from you the sight of your own body in the shadow of his Great Light. I say unto you, as you leave this place of sadness and go upon your way to the land where there is no joy and sadness, where there is no light and darkness, as you walk along this path beyond the stars, may you go with a feeling of peace in your heart. Look not back to your brothers and sisters, we who remain behind in the shadows. Look not back to find once more your brothers and sisters, your parents, old, their hearts filled with sorrow. But look ahead to the Great Peacemaker, *Nanbush*. Say unto him, 'I bring this message to you from those I have left in deep sorrow. They beg you to give them long life; may they be given the full span of years that is given to man; may their days not be cut short as were mine. This they beg of you.'" The mourning period was over.

While grieving her departed sister, Mockwasaka felt the presence of Mechkalanne, standing a respectful distance. When their eyes met, she saw her sorrow reflected in his. She had always pictured the Indian men without remorse, capable of the most heinous acts of cruelty and vengeance, their faces impassive, hiding any inner emotion or turmoil. But Mechkalanne was different. His dark cheeks twitched nervously. He behaved like a man protecting his woman from the stares of the curious villagers. His presence comforted her, and she soon found herself leaning against his warm, broad chest, his strong arms supporting her during her hours of prayer and meditation over Rebecca's grave. Mockwasaka, with her usual resilience, drew strength from the presence of Mechkalanne and his people.

*   *   *   *

A few weeks later, She Bear sat Mockwasaka down to tell her the story of Possum Eater's sister, White Fawn. The girl had left her parents' lodge and run off with a white trapper who lived in a run-down cabin not far from the *Lenapewihituk*. When this *plantscheman* threw White Fawn out of his cabin, she returned, dishonored, to the village. She was driven off, forced to leave her people, and delivered to the banks of the *Mahicanituk* with enough food and clothing to survive in the wilderness. White Fawn, disgraced and in desperation, returned to the Frenchman's cabin. He took her back but was soon abusing her again, beating her up in his drunken stupors. It was not long before White Fawn joined the paleface in his daily drink of firewater.

Soon, the Frenchman threw White Fawn out of his cabin once more. Dissipated, a skeleton of her former self, she showed up near Canopus Hollow where she met up with a bunch of cowboys—white men and Wappinger Indians, and sharing their firewater with them, she fell down drunk with the paleface's poison. She begged for more of the whisky as she and the cowboys stumbled along the side of a road. Pointing to a huge boulder forty feet from top to bottom, one of the men told her that if she jumped from the top of the rock, they would give her another bottle of the bad firewater.

White Fawn, her brain twisted by the poisonous drink, yet craving more, dragged herself to the top of the boulder, leaping to her death far below. Possum Eater, who went in search of his missing sister, found her body and returned with it to the Delaware where she was properly buried. At the burial, he announced to the village that he would seek revenge for what the paleface renegades had done to his sister. When She Bear concluded her story, Mockwasaka realized that the Tidd family had paid dearly for the crime committed against poor White Fawn many years earlier.

Mockwasaka sat at the old woman's feet as She Bear explained the nature of the vengeful act among the Lenape people—that unless a crime such as murder is committed against a sachem or an Indian of high rank—one highly regarded by his people, there is no common law or religious or moral code for punishing the perpetrator. It is the right, however, for close family members to avenge a crime committed against a relative. This was the case with the murder of White Fawn.

The old woman continued.

"The Lenape is a passionate man whose natural feelings are intense—so therefore his passion for revenge is equally intense. However, his tenderness and generosity toward others is as powerful in him as is his desire for revenge. Many Lenape will give their life over for a friend, no matter what his color or his people. A friend, *Elangomat*, equal to a member of his clan, means that the Lenape stands by him in all situations in which this *Elangomat* is in danger or threatened. For this reason, much unneeded bloodshed is prevented among our people. When a Lenape's friendship is put to the test, he never shrinks away in cowardice but is always willing to lay his life on the line. But such friendship is only acquired when the two potential friends treat each other with complete equality."

Mockwasaka did not wish to respond to the old woman's words as is the white man's custom but to mull over in her mind her mother's teachings. She respected her wisdom with the fervor of an Indian.

She Bear concluded.

"It is easy to gain the friendship of a Lenape if one approaches the friendship with good faith and humility. The Indians are especially skilled at reading the faces of others—to learn their real, honest intentions. They immediately sense when they meet a white man if his feeling toward the Indian is a generous feeling or one of scorn and contempt for the color of his skin. They fix their sharp eyes on the face of this potential friend or enemy and can read in his eyes the nature of his soul. This is how the Lenape mark their friends and enemies.

Many white men have double hearts. They are a deceitful race and cannot be trusted; and the Indian often forgets this when he reads only good intentions into the white man's motives for acts of friendship and charity. This is how a treacherous white man, like the trickster spirits among our own *manitowuk*, gains access to our simple hearts. These men are barbarous as are their nations—and the Lenape must keep this thought in their memories when they read for friendship the face of a white newcomer. Once a friend, always a friend until death—this is the nature—the constancy of the friendship offered by the Lenape."

Mockwasaka sat before She Bear, her desire to learn more from the wisdom of the old woman holding her tongue. To speak out at such a time would destroy the moment. This lesson she was eager to absorb. But suddenly she sensed that She Bear had not finished, that she had something else to share with her daughter.

"*Danus.*" She started, then fell silent.

"*Danus.*"

Mockwasaka said nothing.

"*Danus.* Do you value the friendship of our son, your adopted brother, Mechkalanne?"

Her clever eyes searched her daughter's face in the Indian way. The girl felt her face flush.

She was sure She Bear had read her feelings for the handsome young brave, this gentle, passionate man. She looked down to hide the strong feelings which the old woman's question had raised in her heart. She was tongue tied. She looked up into dark eyes.

"I admire Mechkalanne. He is strong, handsome, and he has great courage and nobility."

She looked away.

"But I fear all Lenape men except Black Turtle who is my father now. They have done me and my family terrible wrongs. They are evil."

She chose not to reveal her true feelings toward the future sachem—the hope of his clan for survival after Black Turtle's death—the pride of the old couple—not to reveal to her that Mech's very presence set her heart racing and left a lump in her throat.

The crafty old woman's face fell. She had no knowledge of the violation that her daughter had suffered the night of her abduction, and Mockwasaka had erased the memories of that night from her waking mind—although her dreams were still troubled by the image of the dark phallus—the ripping, tearing organ that ended her childhood and brought the ugly reality of her world down upon her.

She Bear pursued her purpose.

"Mechkalanne has come to Black Turtle and me requesting our permission for him to take you as his wife. He desires Mockwasaka to share his lodge and his life with him. His sincerity is pure. He is a good man. He will give respect to Mockwasaka and comfort and protection to her in her time of grief. He will come to our lodge at our signal of your acceptance of his request—to offer us and Mockwasaka the nuptial gifts."

Her voice trailed off. Her daughter did not respond, but the image of King David popped into her mind. It quickly turned into the half-naked figure of Mechkalanne, the tender eyes of the poet-warrior and the piercing eyes of the Lenape hunter merging into one. She knew that the brave loved her. She began to sob.

"*Gauh! Hase! Gauh! Hase!* I have been violated by one of Possum Eater's braves the night of my capture. My body has been degraded. May God Almighty have mercy on my child's soul!!"

She Bear's face was stricken. Mockwasaka looked down, her eyes red, her body shaking. The old woman pulled her child's trembling body to her. Mock fell into her withered arms.

She held her tight, rocking her back and forth.

She Bear withdrew from the lodge, leaving Mockwasaka alone to entertain the proposal by the kind, generous brave, who always kept his distance, who had shown her nothing but respect and admiration. Her heart was overflowing with conflicted feelings. She wept, in relief, and in sadness. And then she made up her mind. She would accept the young brave and future sachem's offer. She decided then and there that it was indeed her David who had come to her in the guise of a Lenape brave.

*   *   *   *

The midwinter icy blast howled down the *Lenapewihituk*, whirlwinds of fine snow spiraling up and around the towering palisades, drifting against the base of the cliffs, banking against the longhouses, burying many of the smaller domed lodges of the Lenape settlement. The river was frozen shore to shore with thick green-blue ice patches exposed among wind driven snow, drifting into parallel serpentine crusts.

Puffs of white smoke escaped through the holes in the Lenape lodges, whisked away by the icy winds. Fur-covered figures dressed in bear skin parkas, loomed out of occasional white-outs of biting, stinging snow pellets, dark phantoms emerging from the swirling snow clouds. These ghostly figures slipped out of the lodges to reach the little silos—the storage bins next to their dwellings, then disappeared into the snow bound huts. *Achwilowan*—winter, cruel. It was a cruel, hard winter.

Mockwasaka, Black Turtle, and She Bear sat wrapped in their heavy, black bear robes at the edge of the sachem's lodge. The single entrance way was now covered with a wicker and thatch door, reinforced with bear hide—the fatty bear skin an impenetrable insulation for the drafty lodge's exit. The smaller huts with their crowded interiors were warmer than the long houses.

Mock sat crouched, her hair shoulder-length, swept back in two braids, secured by shining mother-of-pearl clasps. She wore a brightly colored, red, black, and blue, mottled, leather skirt and blouse, with elegant, multicolored porcupine quills and beaded moccasins. Her eyes were shining. She smiled nervously at her parents who beamed proudly, awaiting the arrival of Mechkalanne to claim his woman.

She spoke the *Unami* dialect with little hesitation now. She told the old couple of her joy in receiving the hand and gifts of Mechkalanne. She looked forward to spending her days in his lodge. Her husband would still be her adopted brother, her *Elangomat*, her friend of friends.

She thanked them for taking her in when she and Rebecca were at the mercy of the marauders led by black-souled Possum Eater—and of her fear of leaving their lodge. They would be close by—she knew that—but the terror of the abduction was still there. Mechkalanne would surely treat her gently. Her pain at the loss of Rebecca lay deep within her, but he understood her grief and would respect it. His wise spirit would give her space and time to rid her heart of the dark memories of that *Tachwoak*.

Delaware custom did not permit Mechkalanne to court her in the way of the *ingelischman,* and there was no "bundling" as was the custom among the Dutch settlers. The brave soon arrived, his arms filled with nuptial gifts for his bride and for her parents. The old couple bowed slightly, signaling that they accepted and honored the wedding gifts.

They conducted Mockwasaka to Mechkalanne's lodge. They in turn produced gifts of corn, squash, leather pouches, and wicker baskets filled with pottery, ornaments, bead work and clothing, all produced by the skillful hands of She Bear. She also presented Mockwasaka with a cooking pot.

When the time came, Mechkalanne announced his wish to live long and happy with his paleface bride—to honor her and to protect her and their children with his strength and the skills he had gained from his father, Black Turtle, and from the Great Spirit, *Kishelsmukay,* who lived in the twelfth and highest heaven. The old man took each of the couple's hands, urging them to treat each other with kindness and respect.

He looked Mechkalanne squarely in the face, and taking his hand, placed it over Mockwasaka's. He spoke.

"*Nanni lenno wulli lenno*—This man is good-natured; *Tgauchau*—gentle and well-minded; *Wulapeyeiyu*—He is virtuous; *Wulapeuwilleno*—a gentleman; *Schiki lenno*—a fine man, a handsome man; *Metelensit*—a humble man; *Alohow-iwi*—He is loving; *Ktuholuk*—He loves thee."

He turned to the blushing Mockwasaka.

"Mockwasaka—Red-haired woman; *Mochgawale*-Kiss me; *Eluwi Schiki Amimi*—a dove; *Amemens*—a child; *Nitschan*—a child; *Won nnitschan*—This is my child."

He turned to his son, and solemnly placed Mock's hand in Mech's.

"*Wonhnitschan Wikimat*—Your wedded wife; *Wikian al*—Go in thy house."

The sachem and his woman rose with Mechkalanne's gifts in their arms and left, leaving the couple in the warm lodge. They disappeared in a biting white cloud of wind-driven snow pellets to the safety and warmth of their own hut.

Mock looked around her new dwelling, excited, her heart pounding, fearful, blushing. It was the lodge of a great hunter. Mech's hut was equal to Black Turtle's, but warmer. The tiered platform along the walls was draped with furs of all shapes, sizes, and colors from every imaginable animal. From the ceiling hung spears with different shaped points, bows and arrows, and a basket filled with arrowheads and spear tips fashioned from sparkling quartz, dull slate and flint.

She was amazed at the abundance of animal skins and feathers. There were bear skin blankets, the skins tanned to make them soft and supple. There were blankets made from beaver and raccoon. It was mid-winter, and the furs were now worn near the body for added warmth. Mock turned, facing her husband.

He had gone to great lengths to adorn himself, preparing his dress to please her. He was wearing a deer skin shirt, leggings and bearskin moccasins turned inside out, the soft bear fur hugging his feet. His leather shirt's long sleeves and his leggings were ruffled. He was clean shaven, his facial hair plucked out. His head had been shaved except for his cock's comb. A beautiful white feather hung to the side of his head, his bare cheeks painted with animal figures, in dark red and blue. On one cheek, in red, was a hawk's beak, and on the other, in black, the bird's head and eyes. She spotted a tiny white turtle etched on his high forehead—the symbol of his clan.

Glowing with the warmth of his simple, affectionate nature, his eyes reflected great pride in his personal regalia and appearance. He wore a handsome breast plate and around his neck hung a belt of white and silver wampum beads. In his arms he carried a beautiful cloth petticoat dyed red, blue and black. At his side was a wicker basket filled with broaches of mother-of-pearl, and silver ribbons and beads. On top sat a pair of women's moccasins embroidered with dyed porcupine quills, bordered by tiny bells, all the work of the loving hands of She Bear.

Mock blushed as Mech spoke to her.

"*Ktaholell*—Polly Tidd; Mockwasaka, *Ktaholell*—I love thee; *Aptahowaltowagan*—Love unto death; *Wikimat*—My wedded wife."

He lowered his head, handing the nuptial gifts to her, which she accepted.

"You are a good, kind brave, Mechkalanne. I am honored to be your wife. But I am afraid."

Tears welled up in her eyes.

"*Aptahowaltowag*—I am not yet ready."

They were filled with shame and fear.

"*Aptahowaltowag*—I am not yet ready."

He was bewildered, confused. She started to sob. His painted forehead and cheeks reminded her of the ugly face and cruel eyes of her violator. She felt herself sinking into despair—the emptiness—the bottomless pit into which she had been plunged that autumn night.

She leaned back against the side of the lodge, the soft, soothing raccoon fur embracing her. Mech, his fallen face flushed in puzzlement and frustration, stepped back. He regained his composure. He did not understand her reluctance to allow him to come near her.

"*Metschigischuarnallsi?*--Are you warm?"

"I am warm. I am comfortable and happy in your lodge, Mechkalanne."

She touched his bronze cheekbones, grazing his tattooed forehead.

"You're a beautiful man, Mechkalanne."

"And you, Polly Tidd, are a beautiful woman."

He reached out to her, brushing her moist, swollen eyelids. She closed her eyes, slipping into a blissful sleep, her body releasing its tension as it sank into the warmth of the animal furs.

In her dreams, Mock found herself on a broad, pleasant meadow whose soft grasses held her like a babe in a tepid bath. She looked up to see King David approaching her. The image vanished, replaced by an Indian, a strong, tall, naked man—bronzed and shining. He became an eagle, his outstretched wings enveloping her. The strange bird held her tightly in its wingspread, filling her with its strength. Her body came alive, quivering in rhythm to the movements of the great bird. It lifted her up gently. She was soaring. The eagle took her higher and higher. Waves of intense pleasure welled through her, then release—and peace. She was filled, complete. She slept for a long time.

The following day broke clear and calm. The bitter north wind had abated and the Lenape emerged from their lodges, dressed in their heavy bearskin parkas. Small children rushed down to slide on the frozen *Lenapewihituk*. The women left their huts to profit from the mid-winter calm, gathering firewood and provisions from the storage bins. The men, fishing nets and tomahawks in hand, headed down to the river, chopping holes in the thickening ice. They yanked out hungry yellow and white perch one after another. The fish, flopping around on the bare ice, had been lured up to the spudded fishing holes with small grubs cut from their protective, bulbous pods attached to goldenrod stems still standing in the nearby meadows.

There the snow-covered earth had been swept clean by the howling north wind.

Other men followed a creek to a beaver dam and pond, a short distance upstream from the overhanging cliffs. The beavers had built lodges in the banks of the pond. On the bottom, below the frozen surface, there were larger lodges built of sticks and mud. The men carried hand spikes, hatchets and spears to break open hollow air-filled pockets in the ice. Pikes in hand, the men smashed a hole in the beaver lodge. The dispossessed creatures scattered, surfacing to breathe in the holes the Lenape had chopped. The braves grabbed the breathless creatures by their hind legs, hauling them out onto the ice where they were tomahawked.

Returning to the village, their arms filled with the prolific animals, they prayed to the beavers' *Manitowuk*, asking for forgiveness. As soon as the hunters were safely inside their lodges, they pitched a wad of sacrificial tobacco into their fires in thanks to the beavers' brave spirits, which had bestowed upon the Lenape such a bountiful gift.

Mech and his woman spent the night and early morning wrapped in their warm animal furs enjoying their first day of marital bliss. Later the lovers left their lodge, walking hand in hand out across the village, watching the excited children in their games on the icy river, greeting the old men and women. Young couples smiled at them, knowingly. They smiled their joy back at them. Several young women, giggling, approached the newly weds. The first girl to reach them gave Mock the once over. She eyed Mechkalanne, her dark eyes glued to his muscled thighs and crotch.

She shouted to her companions, pointing to his feet.

"*Mechkalanne! Amangi uchsit! Amangi uchsit! Amangi wilackkey! Amang-ilock!*--Mechkalanne! Big feet, big genitals! They are big! They are long!"

As the girl made the appropriate gestures, she shrieked in laughter, her friend imitating her. Mech smiled at the comment. Mock pulled him roughly away to escape the women's searching eyes, delighted with themselves and their observations.

The couple pulled each other playfully along, frolicking in the snow drifts alongside the village children, absorbed in their own play on the ice and in the deepening snow drifts.

Mock whispered in Mech's ear.

"I didn't know the Lenape women were so aggressive!"

"Some Lenape women are free with words and their actions when it comes to things like this. When I was a young boy of twelve winters or so, they would chase me in groups of three or more, and if they caught me, they would pull down my breechclout to examine me down there to see if they had grown and if I was ready to do it as a man. I would run off into the forest like a scared rabbit!!"

Mech laughed. So did Mockwasaka. The lovers walked back to their lodge as the bitter north wind began to rise, howling. They hurried to enter the hut, its warmth, its comforting fur blankets and robes, its half light, its long, endless nights beckoning them in.

Mockwasaka's Dream

King David, her young lover, stood in a bright meadow, singing his praises to the heavens. Mock stood before him. He played his lyre for her pleasure, praising her simple beauty, her gentle soul. She shed her garments, dropping them to her ankles, offering herself to him. He sang sweetly, Mock drawing him to her.

He removed his halter, his handsome face growing dark and bronzed, his cheekbones rising high and prominent. He dropped his protective head gear, revealing a shaved head with a hairlock, a single feather dangling down the side of his head. David, the King, became Mechkalanne, the naked Delaware brave. His phallus, almost black, hung down heavily against a muscled thigh. Mock, at first repelled at the sight, became aroused as the organ began to thicken and lengthen, flaring up, stirring like some strange animal.

Mock awoke from the dream, looking up into the darkened lodge. She glimpsed the silhouette of a tall brave, above her, his eager eyes reflecting her own desire. Her hand dropped to her red bush. Her fingers reached down to touch the lips, parting them, revealing her red cleft which began to swell. She rubbed her pleasure spot gently. Waves of intense pleasure rose up within her, starting at her mount of Venus, radiating out in all directions, down her limbs, climbing up through her buxom body. She opened her eyes wide. She raised her head to see Mechkalanne, the red-skinned savage, his phallus, purplish, brooding, responding to her gesture of submission. It rose quickly, its thick shaft bobbing up, breaking free of its hooded prison. Mech, his object of pleasure in hand, followed it eagerly as it drew him down toward Mock. She spread her lips to receive the hard shaft of the aroused Indian. It penetrated her swiftly, effortlessly. As the lovers' intense joy mounted, they cooed softly, moaning, rocking back and forth, filling the lodge with their sweet song.

Mockwasaka's vision of David was gone, banished from her sleeping and her waking, a transparent fantasy. Mechkalanne, the wise and gentle Indian, flesh and blood, filled her every moment.

*   *   *   *

Mockwasaka and Mechkalanne received Black Turtle's pipe, each taking a long drag, drawing the smoke into their lungs. Mech blew out smoke rings, imitating his father. Mock choked and gagged. The old man laughed. The young couple sat back, leaning against the side of the lodge. And Black Turtle, speaking in a subdued voice, began another one of his tales.

"In the olden days a living spirit was Corn. This was told and retold from time immemorial. The wise sachems knew this to be so and would repeat it regularly to the younger ones.

One cold winter's day, after hearing the tale told the previous night in the lodge of the sachem, White Elk, a group of young boys laughed at the idea of Corn being human-like, making light of the story told by the sachem. One boy scoffed. 'Corn cannot leave Earth. She is here to stay. She is everywhere, in our fields, our lodges.' The following season drought struck—no rain for months, and famine—she quickly followed."

Black Turtle stopped. He grimaced, looking up gravely. The couple fidgeted nervously. He continued.

"The rain dances proved futile—and soon the Corn disappeared—withered away to nothing in the fields. Famine and her companion, Death, stared the *Unami* square in the face.

Then a sachem was blessed by the Great Spirit, who sent him a token in a dream which said to him, 'You must find a person who has gift of tongues and with this power, you can speak with the Corn Spirit to coax Corn to return to us. You must humor the Corn that she might come back to us. Unless you do as I tell you, Corn will not return, and the famine will continue. Once the Corn disappears, its heart will turn into living beings who will sprout wings and take to flight, never to return' The Great Spirit, through this token, explained to the sachem the cause of Corn's departure along with the other vegetables. It was because a group of young men had made uncalled for remarks about the Corn and the Spirit of the Corn."

Mock wondered how Black Turtle could recall each detail of the tale so vividly. Then she remembered the bundle of sticks which he fingered while recounting his story. She had many questions she wanted to ask him about the disappearance of Mother Corn, but she would wait.

Black Turtle continued.

"Therefore, the Great Spirit sent the messenger spirit, the leading spirit, *Misingw,* or 'whole face,' with the token to warn the people of the great wrong the boys had committed in the eyes of the Corn Spirit.

One young and crazy brave stepped forward, and upon hearing the sachem's warning, boldly announced, 'Mother Corn cannot get away from me!'

And then the scornful brave, he filled a deer skin pouch with dried corn, what little remained for the tribe's meager eating, and then as a pillow, he placed the corn-filled pouch under his head each night when he went to sleep. One night he awoke in the middle and realized that the pouch had disappeared out from under his head, that it had taken flight in the form of a giant corn weevil."

The lovers laughed, Black Turtle smiling. Mock's brain was swimming from the powerful effects of the Indian ceremonial tobacco.

Black Turtle, relishing the intense interest he had awakened in the two, continued.

"Who would come forth to help restore Mother Corn and save the *Unami* from certain extinction? The tribe had learned that in their number were two orphan boys who were very poor and lived and survived with even less food than the starving *Unami.* It was a great mystery as to how they could bring Mother Corn back. The people gathered in council, then sent their messengers, (as ordered by the token in another dream), to go fetch the two wretched boys and bring them to the gathering where they were told of the sachem's dream. The two boys were immediately recognized by him as possessing mystic powers, and they offered their services to the *Unami* to help contact the Spirit and to restore Mother Corn.

The people of the village gathered together, sitting in a ring, as the boys prepared for their departure for the region on high to contact the Spirit of Mother Corn. When morning came, the boys were gone, leaving no clue as to how they managed to reach the region above where the Spirit of Mother Corn lived. When they reached her new abode in the sky, they presented a mussel shell as a sacrificial burnt offering for the return of Corn. Upon hearing the boys' request, Mother Corn announced she would return. The boys then came back to their people, bringing the good news and a handful of corn as a token from Corn and her pledge never to leave again."

"How did the boys convince Mother Corn to return?"

Black Turtle looked up, no longer gazing at the bundle of sticks. His eyes twinkled.

"Tell us! Tell us! Black Turtle!"

"When the boys arrived in the region above, they found Spirit Corn in the form of an aged woman, scabby and withered, which meant they had mistreated her when she was on Earth.

Mother Corn said, 'When I was dry and parched, my children treated me badly. They should have handled me differently, more gently. They should have kept me moist and not let me get so dry and parched. They could have rubbed tallow on me.' At first, Mother Corn refused to return to Earth, but when the boys offered to sacrifice the shells, she wanted to participate in the offering. But they refused to allow Mother Corn to partake unless she agreed to return to Earth. She finally consented."

Black Turtle was nearing the end of his tale, ready to conclude with a lesson for them, and for their children and for their children's children—to the seventh generation.

"It was the Great Spirit's will that Corn would live in the far heavens as an old woman who ruled over all vegetation. This custom originated with our ancestors long before the paleface came to this continent and centuries thereafter. This is why we know that Corn was here when the white man discovered this land. The handfuls of Corn that the poor boys brought back to Earth with them were divided among the Indian peoples until Corn was once more restored to the continent. Since Mother Corn took the image of a woman, it became our custom to hand the care and culture of the Corn over to the women, who tenderly care for the Corn, dressing neatly when they plant the corn seed and when they cultivate it in the fields and even when they are husking it."

Mock was delighted with the tale's climax and Black Turtle's conclusion. Mech puffed on Black Turtle's pipe. The old man grunted.

"Do you believe in ghosts, Black Turtle?"

"What are ghosts, my child?"

"You know, the spirits of the dead that walk on the Earth among us."

Black Turtle nodded and began another tale.

"Some Minsi men left their village one day in search of the dead. They wanted to know where their spirits went after leaving the bodies of the living. They traveled towards the the south for many suns. And finally, they came to some camps and houses that looked newly constructed.

The long houses and their lodges were all well swept out and cared for, but there were no people to be seen anywhere around the village. The men peeked inside each lodge and the longhouse, but they were empty. Then the men decided to wait until nightfall, so they camped out in the center of the deserted village, careful not to disturb the dwellings of the settlement.

When night fell, the village suddenly came alive with voices of talking and laughter.

There were people everywhere in the dark, and from one lodge a drum could be heard. The Minsi visitors mixed with these people as was their custom and spent the night enjoying themselves. One of the braves even found a good-looking woman from the village, a woman with dark eyes, a gentle spirit, and with a voice as soft as a dove's breast. This woman did not have a man, so our brave took a fancy to her. She invited him into her lodge where they spent the evening together filling each other's ears with wonderful music."

Mockwasaka's and Mechkalanne's eyes met, exchanging a spark of desire. They smiled awkwardly, their eyes cast down to avoid meeting the old sachem's knowing smile.

He continued. "That night the young brave decided he wanted to marry this beautiful, gentle spirit, but when he went to her parents' lodge to ask permission to take the woman in marriage, they told him it could not be done because they were all dead people—spirits come from the living.

Since the brave was a living man, he could not dwell with them but would have to return to the land of the living. The visitors finally fell asleep in the middle of the village, and when they awoke the following morning at daylight, the spirits were gone—there was no one to be seen or heard, and the village was as empty and abandoned as the moment they had arrived the previous day.

The travelers then set out to return to their village, happy to leave the world of the dead behind and to return to the land of the living—that is, all except the young brave who loved the ghost woman. His mind and heart, he left behind in the ghost village even though his young body walked with his brothers on the trail leading back to their village.

When the band approached within an arrow's flight of their lodges, they had to cross a deep river on a rope bridge. All proceeded across with the love-lost brave at the rear of the file. He was pining after the young woman's spirit. Midway across, the youth threw himself off the bridge into the torrent below, disappearing in the foam. He had joined the spirit of the dead woman he loved that he had to leave behind."

Black Turtle lowered his head, awaiting Mech's customary grunt of approval. Mock brushed a tear from her cheek. The sachem nodded, acknowledging the couple's pleasure with his story.

Silence reigned in the sachem's lodge. Mock's thoughts turned back to the Gamwing celebration of the previous *Tachwoak.*

"*Noch*—my father, Black Turtle, tell us your dream vision so that we can relive those moving moments of *Gamwing.* The Great Spirit certainly spoke through your words the first night of *Engamwing.*"

The north wind whistled, then howled around the sachem's lodge, confirming his daughter's request, the wind's bitterness adding to her desire to remain a while longer in the sachem's lodge. Mech smiled, nodding.

Black Turtle hesitated, but only for a second. A Lenape story teller never misses the opportunity such a request invites. He began to chant, his voice rising slowly, the words soon flowing without hesitation. He puffed on his pipe, blowing one large smoke ring towards the open hole in the peak of the lodge. For a second, Mock thought she saw his very words taking shape in the ascending smoke rings.

"In the beginning, I lived in the land of the Turtles, the *Unami,* those Lenape who lived to the south—not far from the Great Water that ebbs and flows. My Mother, White Turtle, through her wisdom and age, protected me for all time, far beyond our days. Her Children, the Wind, the Rain, the Sun and the Moon are my Brothers and Sisters. She taught us to build our lodges strong to face our Brother Wind when he grew angry.

White Turtle, my Mother, came from the East and returned to the East, leaving us on the shore with our white wampum and our shells. In my first memory, I hear her voice singing to us. She sang to us that her Sister, Mother Earth, had called her back to the Eastern Sea, from whence she came, but that she would return to carry us to safety if we ever were in danger and we called on her for help. My Father, White Otter, swam with her in the blue waters. Swimming together, they taught me the strong kick I would need if the waters ever came to surround us."

Black Turtle fell silent, inhaling deeply. The smoke rings filled the lodge, rising, dancing above their heads. Mock was drunk now from the ceremonial tobacco smoke and from the sachem's words. The couple sat patiently awaiting the conclusion of Black Turtle's vision.

"And the waters rose, and they did come and swept away our dwellings, our strong Turtle lodges, and I was in the water struggling, and White Otter, my Father, swam under the water like the teal, the wild duck, diving deep and warning my Mother, White Turtle, of our danger; and White Turtle, she rose from the depths of the Great Water, swimming quickly to my side while I was floundering, sinking into the rolling, shaking froth of the Great Water, the same froth from which the Great Manito created the paleface."

The sachem turned, smiling at his daughter.

"And White Turtle, my Mother, swam up from the deep Great Water and came to my side, (I was just a small thing), lifting me up on her white shell, saving me from the dark waters. As she rose high above the waters, she turned her long, thin neck and faced me. With her glittering eyes glowing with love, intelligence and great wisdom, she named me 'Black Turtle' because like the turtle, I had risen out of the darkness.

And then she begged me.

'Black Turtle, my son, you are now safe from the waters. Go north to the hill people, the *Munsi*, the Wolf people, and be with them. They are in distress and suffering from the Evil Spirits, the Tricksters, brought to the Lenape by the White Man from the East—the Man we welcomed with open arms—the Man we thought was the Son of *Manitu* returning to us. The *Minsi* are suffering from smallpox, the paleface's disease, and the poisonous firewater which he brought to destroy our people. Go to the black, hardened souls among our people who have been injured by the long knives—the paleface warriors. Go to your brothers, the *Minsi,* and be with them to help them survive. I will return to you at the appointed Moon to complete my mission to you."

Here the vision ended, the sachem casting his eyes to the ground.

Mockwasaka rubbed her swollen stomach tenderly as she lay in the soft embrace of the bearskin throws covering her naked body. She thought she detected a faint fluttering within her protruding belly. The bouts of nausea from which she had been suffering for weeks had passed. All she could think about was the tart cranberries and crabapples from the previous harvest which She Bear had squirreled away in the little storage silo sitting before the sachem's lodge and which she so desperately wanted to taste. Sunshine from the growing spring season entered through the open entrance to their lodge, casting a new radiance on her rosy complexion. A tepid spring breeze chased the sun rays into Mech's lodge.

She had first felt the nausea after a day of planting in the Lenape corn field with She Bear and Black Turtle. Spring planting had arrived, and the younger braves, along with Mechkalanne, were fishing for the first trout of the season, at their spawning beds in the small streams flowing into Mother Delaware. Meanwhile, the women and the older men had begun an ancient ritual.

They were planting corn in hills dug lovingly in the last stretch of fertile soil, a short distance down river from the Lenape settlement. Mock followed close behind Black Turtle as they dug holes, dropping two or three corn kernels in each. She Bear, carrying a bucket of dead fish, completed the ritual. She carefully placed one in each hole, filling it up with the soft soil. The stench from the rotting fish made Mock retch. As the trio completed each stage of the planting, they chanted songs honoring Mother Corn and calling on her to bless their sowing and their harvest.

She Bear, in her deep monotone, chanted a prayer.

"Mother Corn of our fields, and our Mother *Lenapewihituk,* will you have pity on our poor souls? Will you bless us with your warm sun and gentle rain? For are we not your children? To whom do we belong if not to you? We are your seeds. You have planted us here. Whose seeds are we? To you alone do we belong. To our Mother alone do we belong. We are the children of Mother Corn."

Mock repeated She Bear's oration, imitating the old woman's chant, her neck muscles slightly tensed. The two women swayed back and forth, moving down each row between the hills of newly sown corn, chanting, first in unison, then in counterpoint.

"With great reverence, we move among the flowers. We go singing and dancing among the flowers. The berries ripen. The fruit ripens. Soon the corn ripens."

When the day's planting was done, mother and daughter sat in the refreshing shade of a red cedar tree not far from the corn field, close to the banks of the rushing *Lenapewihituk.* Behind them the river roared in its spring freshet. Mock chanted a final prayer to Mother Corn and to Grandmother Bear, a prayer She Bear had taught her.

"Our Grandmother Bear, our Mother Corn, all of the spirits of our women ancestors, and the spirits of the women to follow us—we beg you! Give us, mother and daughter, *Danus* and *Gauh, Hase,* give us long life together. Take me not until my hair is grey and frosted."

She raised her eyes to the sky.

"Take me not until my hair is grey and frosted. Until that time, may we live this life that we know now. This life is all we know."

Mock, rising to her feet beneath the cedar tree, suddenly sat down hard on the river bank. A wave of intense nausea set her retching. She bent to the ground, vomit shooting out. She Bear came quickly to her side, bending her over. Mock continued to retch and vomit. The old woman questioned her new daughter's malady, her quizzical, wrinkled face broken in a half-smile, suspecting, praying that she was with child. During the days which followed, Mock's bouts of nausea confirmed her suspicions and her greatest hopes.

And now, Mock lay in Mechkalanne's lodge, leaning back, supporting herself against the tiered platform. She Bear crouched before her big stew pot, carefully stirring its contents. Mock turned to Mechkalanne lying at her side. He drew her to him, holding her firmly in the cradle of his muscular arm, her braids trailing across his bare chest. Early spring warmth had come to the river valley, and Mock's flushed face reflected her discomfort. She drifted off.

It was the season to carry the cooking pot, utensils, and cooking fire outside the lodge to relieve its occupants from the rising heat. This Mech and She Bear were quietly discussing as she continued to stir the contents of the stew pot.

He had been out collecting greens, the first spring seedlings, for She Bear's hearty soup, whose delicious broth he awaited with his infinite patience. Tender dandelion sprouts, seedlings of wild mustard and watercress, had been cooked separately, and now the old woman was stirring in pink trout meat, which Mech had caught early that morning and roasted on a spit outside the lodge. The savory odor from the cooking potage wafted up Mock's nose, stimulating her many cravings. Hunger jarred her awake, and startled, she let out a deep sigh, settling back into Mech's warm embrace.

*   *   *   *

Mother Corn had kept her word. She had given the Lenape people, reverent and prayerful in her presence and before her supreme power, many *Tachwoaks* of abundant harvests. But the fertile soil along the banks of the Delaware was spent. And in spite of an early spring and plentiful rainfall and sunshine, the villagers' corn fields stood sparse, half their normal height.

Mock's belly grew rounder, protruding more and more. The corn stalks grew thinner, drooping. The villagers prepared for an early harvest. They spread out over their ancient fields, gathering what corn they could salvage, chanting their prayers and songs to Mother Corn.

Meanwhile, Black Turtle had disappeared into his lodge. For many suns the old man sat crouched in the darkness, deep in prayer, chanting softly. Mock entered his hut one day in search of Mechkalanne and found the sachem at the rear, his eyes closed, listening intently.

When he emerged from his meditation, he summoned Mechkalanne.

"Go tell all our people to come to my lodge. I have important words to tell them."

"Yes, sachem!"

The urgent tone of the old man's command set Mech running through the village, along the banks of the river, to the distant corn and bean fields where the villagers were working. Soon women, braves, children, old and young, stood before the sachem's lodge, eager to hear his words. Mock felt a tension rising from the silent crowd. She sat beside Mechkalanne, her hands resting on her large stomach. The solemnity of the moment troubled her. She was very large now, and the day of the birth of their child was near.

A few days earlier, She Bear had pulled her aside, placing a drooping ear against her daughter's belly, listening. She turned her around, her sharp eyes scanning Mock front and back.

Observing the way her belly stuck out, she announced proudly.

"Mock is carrying a son!"

She accepted the old woman's observation as received directly from the mouth of the Great *Nanabush* himself. Later, when she whispered the news to Mechkalanne, the brave beamed proudly.

Now she sat before the sachem's lodge, waiting, worried. When Black Turtle, followed by She Bear, emerged from the darkened hut, his face was grave. He began to speak, the villagers falling silent, except for the "shushing" of excited children. They did not want to miss a single word. She Bear backed away from the sachem.

He stood.

"Turtle people, Wolf people. I have summoned the spirit of my clan—White Turtle—my spiritual mother. Her voice joins together with the voice of Mother Corn—her vision, my vision. After my days of prayer, White Turtle has come to me in a dream as she promised many summers ago when she beckoned me to come to the land of the *Minsi* people.

Our Mother Turtle has spoken in a bright, clear vision. She has shown me our clan, our braves, the old men, the women and children, our weapons, our tools, our traps—the gifts which we have received from Mother *Lenapewihituk*—given to us so generously—as we begin a journey into the sun to a new home on the banks of the *Siskuhanawak,* the muddy waters.

Mother Corn awaits our arrival before *Tachwoak* and the hunt. Many of our peoples will be there to welcome as did our ancestors in olden times. We must abandon our Mother Delaware. She is ready to let us go, to fly like a fledgling hawk. We must finish gathering our corn, squash, and beans.

Let us give thanks to Mother Delaware for her gifts to us over the many winters we have lodged on her banks—for her abundance, her generosity with her fish, their brother beaver, *Machk*—our Grandfather Bear, *Achtu*—the quick-to-leap deer—all our Manitowuk that have lived with us and have treated us generously.

Let us pray to them and the Great Spirit, *Nanabush*, that they will join us, that they will not abandon us as did Mother Corn of old—that they will stay close beside us until we reach the banks of the *Siskuhanawak*—to join our Lenape brothers, our cousins, the *Shawuno*, and the *Susquehannocks*, the Muddy River people, and all of our ancestors who once lived there and the country beyond."

Black Turtle lowered his head. He did not tell his people his one fear—that the paleface long knives and their brethren would be waiting for them along the banks of the *Siskuhanawak.*

It was indeed a solemn moment. Mock looked up at Mech, her face set in a frown. He placed his hand on her protruding belly. They sat in silence. Finally, he spoke.

"Our son will begin his life in a new land. Let us pray, Mock, that it is a bountiful one—that the hunt is plentiful—the rivers full of fish and that Mother Corn is standing near the river bank awaiting our arrival, as Black Turtle has promised."

Mock did not understand the urgency of the moment and what such an exo-dus meant to her adopted people. All she knew was that she was scared—that her child was due any day—that she was miserably uncomfortable in late summer heat—and that her new family—*Wuski Guttangunditschik*—she called them, were uprooting her just as her roots had begun to take hold in the soil of the *Lenapewihituk*. She began to weep, large tears forming in the corners of her eyes, their salty film blurring the grim face of Mech above her.

Her large belly was shaking.

"I'm frightened, Mech—*Wipalukgun, Notschihillachsi.* I am exhausted. Our son is coming. I am heavy with child. And what about the long knives and their militia? What will become of me if they come upon us and they spot my red hair and pale face? They will surely seize me and drag me back with them to one of their forts!"

Mechkalanne placed his hands tenderly on Mock's shoulder, her frown extending down to her full lips. She resembled those scowling face masks staring down from the door posts and columns of the Big House.

"Do not worry, my Mock. I will be at your side throughout our journey. I will protect you from any long knives or renegades we meet on the trail. And it will take our people only a few suns to reach our new homeland. Mother Corn has prepared it for us. She will greet us with pleasure on her face when we arrive on the banks of the *Siskuhanawuk.*"

For the moment he had assuaged her fears.

She felt threatened for her unborn child while Mechkalanne exuded his usual confidence—the hope and joy of the hunter about to cross into new hunting land—like the Red Hawk—his *Manitowuk*—alert, ever ready, its fleeting eyes surveying a newly discovered field of prey.

"Mechkalanne will lead the way for Mockwasaka and our son. My brothers will be waiting for us. I will quickly find my cousins for the kill. My Turtle Grandmother and our Grandfather Bear will be at my side, guiding my quick hawk eyes to their targets."

He patted Mock's sagging shoulders.

"I am sorry. I am troubled,--*Nschiwelendam Ni Schiwamallsin.*"

It was the end of *Nipen*. Early harvest completed, their hearth fires extin-guished, their final prayers of thanksgiving offered to Mother Delaware, the *Minsi* people, the *Unami* at the lead, chanted a long, ritual oration of farewell, as they slowly, in pairs and in single file, began the trek up the western slopes of the Delaware River bottom, winding their way up sharp ravines, like the ones Polly

Tidd, Rebecca and their captors had descended more than two years earlier. They forded the river an arrow's flight upstream from the abandoned village, beyond a large bend, at a point where the river widened in a shallow expanse, soon losing themselves in the dense forest.

They were repeating the migration west, begun many years earlier by their Delaware brothers and sisters, their cousins, the Shawnee, and the *Mengwe*, the tribes who refused to submit, unwilling to share their territory with the growing hordes of paleface settlers. Now, they too, one of the last clans of the Lenape on the *Lenapewihituk*, were traveling to the far reaches of their domain—to the limits of the Delaware lands, territory agreed upon with the *Mengwe*, their old allies turned enemy, territory now controlled by the strange laws of the paleface.

The terrain here was flatter, less rocky and mountainous than the trails which led from the Hudson to the Delaware. Their destination was the upper Susquehanna. Black Turtle knew that the exodus would be more difficult than that of the people who had gone before them.

Their ancestors had battled the *Taligawe* alongside their cousins, the Mengwe, and the Lenape had prevailed. Now the Lenape, along with their cousins, the Shawnee, were fleeing from the paleface soldiers and the *angelishmen* squatters. The settlers were intent on clearing the Lenape hunting lands to plant their crops. The Lenape's brothers, the deer, bear, and beaver, had joined them in their flight before the advancing white men.

These waves of new peoples, led by their long knives soldiers, and the growing colonial militia, these treacherous paleface warriors, Black Turtle knew, would steal from the *Lenni Lenape*, the original people, what little territory was left.

He was leading the *Minsi* into a country in conflict—contested by many nations—their cousins, the *Mengwe*, and the whites migrating up the great river from the south, in search of furs and land.

And they kept coming, bringing with them their poisonous firewater and their smallpox. He knew the land his clan had to cross was filled with dangers as it had been for his grandfathers when they had crossed it hundreds of years earlier; but it had taken them in,--protecting them and offering safe passage—long ago when they fought the *Talligawes* to reach Sassafras land—that kind, generous, once abundant land they now had to leave behind.

Mock walked a few steps behind Mechkalanne, his back straining as he dragged a litter charged with furs, cooking pots and utensils, and bags filled with newly picked corn, beans, and squash. The small children, trailing behind the men and women, carried their share of lighter implements. Too small to drag the

litters, they tended to the dogs bounding playfully through the forest, excited by strange odors to sniff out.

The new-born were bundled up in light animal skins at the front of each litter, or carried on their mothers' backs. There were many this late summer season—the product of the hunters' return the preceding *Tachwoak* and of the long nights spent in their darkened lodges during *Lawilowan*. The infants looked like large dolls with their round faces, shining black eyes, and straight black hair. Their dark cheeks appeared painted with blush. A few hung at their mothers' sagging breasts.

Mock struggled with the weight of her unborn child. Her large protruding stomach and the daily kicks within had convinced her that She Bear's prediction was right—that she was carrying a male child. Sweat poured down her face, her thick red hair braided, wrapped in two buns on top, secured by two mother-of-pearl clasps. The file of migrating Indians moved quickly along a trampled trail, soon breaking out onto a level plain.

Mock's thoughts turned back to the nightmare of the kidnapping—recalling those nights and that awful march from Canopus Hollow to the Delaware. She remembered her fatigue and her feeling of hopelessness. The physical challenge of this moment, in spite of her being heavy with child, paled in comparison.

She was happy to be under the wings of Mechkalanne—a member of his clan—in search of a new home. She thought about the hunter's confidence that they would soon find one. If Black Turtle and his son had doubts or fears about what awaited them on the banks of the Susquehanna, she could not read it on their stoic faces. They exuded nothing but hope and a faith that *Nanabush* would provide for them.

Her anxiety was coupled by her sorrow at leaving for good the remains of Rebecca on the banks of the Delaware. It was her final farewell to her sister. She had visited the grave for the last time early that morning long before sunrise. She said her prayers aloud before her sister's tomb, sure that Rebecca's spirit heard them.

At the crack of dawn, as the villagers gathered before the sachem's lodge to begin the journey west, she was still at the grave side, praying for the family she had left behind and for her new family. Many of her words she had learned from Mechkalanne.

"Oh Great Spirit, *Nanabush*, creator of all things. Dear God, Lord Jesus. Hear my words. May your spirits, great and small, and the lesser spirits, the *Manitowuk* which surround us," (she thought of all the angels), "also hear my words—if it is your wish. Thank you for bringing me, the child I carry, Mechkalanne, Black

Turtle, and She Bear to this place. Lead our bodies, our minds, and our spirits across the wilderness to our new home at the edge of *Talligawe* land. May all the spirits, those of my brother, Aaron, and my sister, Rebecca, go before me. And may they protect my mother and father, Esther and Jacob Tidd. Take them all in your arms, oh Lord and Savior, Jesus Christ, and *Nanabush,* Grandfather of all sentient beings. Lead us safely through the land of our enemies. Protect my unborn child with your powerful medicine. May they all hear my pleas. May they not abandon me and my child on the long march to the *Siskuhanawuk.* Hear me now. May thy will be done. Amen. *Nanne leu.* By the will of Almighty God. *Untschi getannittowit titchewagan.*"

She bowed down, tears flowing freely down her sunburned, flushed face.

Camp fires burned brightly as *Unami* and *Minsi* sat crouched around several large blazes, forming a circle. Oak trees, thick with green acorns, rose protectively above them, the eyes of the fires blinking alive in the dwindling twilight. It would take three grown men, standing arm to arm, to encircle one of these giants of the virgin forest. A pair of grazing deer, their darkening fur illuminated by the crackling flames, emerged from the woods, their white tale flags switching up and down nervously.

Near the center of the circle sat Mockwaska and her clan, their backs supported by a lean-to rigged from the litter Mech had been dragging. The litter was turned on its side, filled with its contents of fur, implements and weapons. They sat with their legs crossed, except for Mock, who lay reclined, her mound of a stomach hiding from view the blazing fire and the wrinkled, flame-reddened face of She Bear. She craned her neck, searching for the old woman. Spotting her, she relaxed.

The Indians sat listening intently to the silence, the softness of the summer night, interrupted by the occasional cry of a hoot owl, the insistent music of wood crickets and the crackling of fire brands bursting open in the warm, moist stillness. She Bear was silent, deep in thought. Finally she spoke, her words chasing away Mock's discomfort.

"My vision is bright, many-colored and far-reaching, like the wing spread of my Father Eagle and the roaming of our Grandmother Bear. My vision begins, like that of Black Turtle, to the south of the *Unami* many winters ago. Mother Bear kept us safe in our huts near the Chesapeake Water. She taught us to hunt far and wide along the banks of the lower *Lenapewihituk* and the shores of the Chesapeake. Mother Bear taught our eyes to look where only bear eyes can see— to search for our brothers and sisters, the White Sturgeon, lying in the depths of the river bay. She taught us to rake up the *Ehes,* clams and mussels lying hidden in the coves and inlets of the dying *Lenapewihituk* as she was swallowed up by the Chesapeake Water. With our sharp gathering claws, we collected the *Ehes,* cracked them open, took their dwellers from them, wolfing them down, carefully saving their mother-pearl houses for wampum beads. Then we prayed to these creatures' *Manitowuk,* thanking them for their sacrifice, begging them to forgive our boldness in removing them from the protective arms of their mother, *Lena-pewihituk.* We learned to trade these wampum beads, gifts from mother Delaware, before she died away into the deep of the endlessly flowing waters, to trade them with our brother Lenape, the *Minsi,* and the *Unalachtigo,* for fur, warm robes, and game from their forests—to sustain us through *Lawilowan,* powerful, unrelenting.

My Father Eagle, along with the paws of our Grandmother Bear, gave me sharp eyes and talons to catch the silver fish swimming up the *Lenapewihituk* L each spring. I was given in marriage to Black Turtle by my mother, Bear Eyes, and my father, Bright Eagle Claws, as Black Turtle visited our village on his journey to the land of the *Minsi.* My dream vision, empowered by that of Grandmother Bear and the far-reaching eyes of Father Eagle, stretches from the shores of the endlessly flowing waters of the *Mahicanituk,* thence to the swiftly flowing waters of the *Lenapewihituk,* finally to the banks of the *Siskuhanawuk* and the *Talligawa* Land beyond."

Mockwasaka, taken with She Bear's vision, broke in, her discomfort gone, her chance to hear her mother's dream vision finally at hand.

"*Ngahuwesenna,* our Mother. *Gahowes!* Tell us about our Grandmother Bear, her uncommon wisdom, her strength, her endurance, and her healing powers! Did she visit you in your dream vision?"

SHE BEAR'S DREAM VISION

"In my dream I am a small girl lost in the dense forest. A she bear and her playful cubs find me and adopt me. Playing with the bear children, I quickly learn to speak their bear language. I learn many things from Bear Mother, many skills which I have passed on to Mechkalanne: how to avoid spreading telltale vapors on the hunt, which the creatures quickly detect and then run away; how to gain the power to kill any game. She Bear taught me that knowledge is power. When I grew up and was ready to leave Mother Bear's lodge, she came up to me, and reaching her hairy bear paws about me, she hugged me closely to her. Then she put her bear mouth against my mouth and said,

'Since my fur body, fur arms, fur paws have touched your body, my power will make you great; it will be a blessing to you.' Her bear paws encircled my shoulders; and then she drew them down my arms, brushing them against my hands; and then she took my hands in her she-bear paws and held them and said, 'With my hands touching your hands, I have made you great, removing all fear from your heart. I have rubbed my paws over you so that you shall be as tough as I am. Because my mouth has touched your mouth, you shall be made wise. I name you *Nunscheach,* She Bear.'"

Mock stretched her feet and distended belly straight towards the fire and in the direction of She Bear's voice. Mech raised up, pressing his cheek against Mock's lily white belly, listening intently to the kicks within. Mock was happy to have finally caught a glimpse of She Bear's former world. What a powerful vision, she thought. The time would surely come when she, in her turn, would share her own dream vision with her new people and with her children, and now She Bear's dream was a part of her dream.

Suddenly, Mechkalanne jumped up from his listening post, his left cheek and ear deep red from pressing them tightly against his child's safe place. He laughed heartily.

"My son kicked me in the cheek! My son kicked me in the cheek! Shall we call him 'Kicking Cheek?'"

Peals of laughter filled the woods.

The trail had been long, heat waves dancing before Mock's bleary eyes. Her face and lips were swollen. So were her legs and feet. She was sure she looked like one of those bloated, dead fish she had seen rising to the surface of the Hudson. While Mech scouted ahead with the other Lenape braves, She Bear stayed close by her side.

The mid-afternoon heat was intense as the party stopped near a stream. There on the banks of the *Walinkpapeek*, the "deep, still water," not far from the *Lechauhannek*, they drank and rested while Mech and his braves headed further down the trail to find a camp site for the rapidly approaching late-summer night. As Mock lay back against a large rock to support her aching body, she felt a wrenching pain down below. A cramp, she thought. A clear liquid erupted from between her legs, spotted with bits of pink.

"She Bear! She Bear! Come quickly!"

The old woman, who had been preparing corn cakes to renew the weary migrants' strength, rushed quickly to her side. Her time had come.

"Mechkalanne! Mechkalanne!"

"He has gone ahead to make sure the way is clear."

Mock tried to stand up but fell backwards, her behind throbbing as it met the hard pillow of the boulder. She Bear pushed her back against the rock, lifting her deer skirt high, up over her head, spreading apart her swollen legs. Her wrinkled hands probed her bulging belly. Its shape had changed. The bulge had dropped much lower. Mock began to moan.

The old woman cried out to one of the other women to fetch fresh water from the nearby stream from which they had been filling water jugs for the rest of the day's trip. There was no time to build a fire to heat the water. Mock was rocking back and forth against the boulder, emitting sharp, whimpering sounds. Like a wounded dog, she kept yipping. Then a long, gurgling shriek rose from the depths of her bloated body.

She Bear pulled her daughter up off her stone bed. Propping her behind against Mock's back, she forced her forward into a squatting position. Bracing her body with one hand, she reached into a small bag she carried around her middle, pulling out a clean bearskin blanket, placing it under her daughter's spread-eagled legs.

"*Ginschtschennemen! Ginschtschennemen!* Push! Push!"

She lodged against Mock's side, rocking forward and backward in a rhythmical movement, urging her to join in her strange dance. She mimicked Mock's moaning, drawing in long breaths, ejecting them with all the force her old body could muster, coaxing her daughter to do the same.

Mock finally managed to imitate She Bear's breathing, and the two women, one very old, one very young, moaned and rocked back and forth together, and then there was a "snap," like the breaking of a thick green tree branch, followed by the first labored cry in that gasp for the breath of life. A bloodied head, covered with black hair, and a swollen red face slipped out. Mockwasaka fell back against the rock, She Bear following her, her wrinkled bloodied hands holding up for Mock to see a squirming, mucous-covered wailing being.

"*Gischiku, gischiku!* He is born! He is born!"

SISKUHANAWAK

When the exhausted Indians dragged themselves, one by one, out of their canoes, onto the shores of the Big Island, in the middle of the Susquehanna, they found a Lenape village abandoned. Mechkalanne held his right hand up above his head, shielding his followers' eyes from the scene lying before them. The former inhabitants' campfires had long since died away, their grey embers scattered by the wind, their huts' thatched roofs gone.

Mockwasaka couldn't believe her eyes. It was like some kind of hellish nightmare she could never imagine except for the sermons of one of the Dutch Calvinist preachers who came to visit their little church back in Peekskill and spent the whole of a Sunday morning preaching hell and damnation—his hell a brutish one full of fire and brimstone, stinking to high heaven with the burning souls of the damned. For a second she thought she detected the smell of burnt sulfur and the moaning of the dead, then realized it was the whining of the wind.

She drew back in horror, pulling Little Bear's tiny body close to her own, covering his wide almond-shaped eyes with her two hands, as if the new-born child could fathom the meaning of the scene. Skeletons, some intact, others, their bones shattered into white shards, lay before each of the still standing huts—those that had not caved in on themselves. All that remained of one lodge was a pile of kindling wood and thatch, tinted with bits of the white bones of its former dwellers.

Skeletons lay in rows, placed there carefully by loving hands. Others leaned against the thatched walls of the huts, scattered about the deserted village, their empty skulls grinning grins of remorse. A few were tiny—those of new-borns and infants. Next to them lay longer ones—two to three feet in length. One had assumed a fetal position in its final death throes.

Mech recognized the scene—a scene all too familiar to him. They had been visited by the great leveler of kings and the common man—of the Lenape and his brothers and sisters. It was the horrible scourge the paleface had brought with him to the land of the Lenape many winters earlier.

"*Despehell*—smallpox. A gift from the white man. Do not touch any of the remains. Stay back!"

He grimaced. Mock reached down, turning Little Bear's inquisitive face away from the death camp. From the rear of the throng came a voice.

"The Big Island is not our final destination as I had thought."

Black Turtle signaled to his band of followers to turn back to their canoes.

"The Big Island is not our final destination. We must move on. Mother Corn has another plan for us."

He was haggard and worn. He struggled to get through the crowd of his followers, their faces reflecting the horror of the scene. His steps uneven, he stumbled. She Bear, following close behind, caught hold of one of his wrinkled arms with one hand.

Mech reached his exhausted parents, slipped between them, wrapping his arms around their thin, bony hips.

"We will rest here for the night and return to the far shore at sunrise. Mother Corn has other plans for our people."

The clan spent the chilly, early fall night on a river bank on the shore of the Big Island, in the middle of the Susquehanna, an island of the dead.

*   *   *   *

Little Bear returned to the Lenape camp at *Sheshequin*, heading across the deserted village toward the hut of Black Turtle and She Bear, two dogs following close at his heels. The lead dog, his constant companion, was *Moekannetit*, Whelp of a Dog, with his pointed, little ears, and his sad, obedient eyes. *Moek* was followed by one of the village strays, an emaciated bag of bones, its ribs sticking out, yapping. It nosed the extinguished fire in front of the ruined cabin.

The stray approached *Moek*, cautiously sniffing his behind. Whelp of a Dog's pointed ears flattened, his sharp fangs bared, his skinny tail lowered. He turned back to face his tormentor, snapping at him menacingly, then turned to heel next to Little Bear's bare leg. The stray stole a final sniff before running off.

When he reached the shack, Little Bear found its only door ajar. Peering in, he found an impenetrable darkness. Commanding *Moek* to sit and stay next to a pile of dead embers, he pulled aside the sagging front door, held in place by one hinge, stepping into the darkened hut. Black Turtle was dozing on a small cot at the back, his body as bony as the stray dog's. She Bear was no where in sight.

Little Bear could make out Black Turtle's form as the old man slowly lifted himself up on the cot, placing his bare feet gently on the dirt floor. They reminded the boy of a skeleton's feet.

"Are you awake, *muchomes*, my grandfather? May I enter?"

Black Turtle spotted his grandson, his face broadening in a big smile. Little Bear was happy to see the old man stir awake. Perhaps he had another tale to tell him. Black Turtle squinted, his dull, failing eyes finally recognizing the boy's silhouette outlined in the shaft of light pouring in through the open door. He motioned to him, clearing his throat.

"Come in! Come in! Enter, my grandchild. *Wikia pal, nachwis.*Your face is happy, glad, as usual, Little Bear. Your eyes, like those of your little brother, Bright Eyes, speak of joy and gladness. Black Turtle welcomes you to his lodge."

He looked around sadly at the shabby interior of the hut.

Little Bear turned to warn away *Moek* as he nosed his way through the half-open cabin door behind his master. "Back! *Ktuckill!*"

The stray dog was back, following close on *Moek's* heels, intent on stealing another sniff of his behind as *Moek* lowered his tail, growling menacingly. The boy started to apologize to the sachem for the two dogs' bad manners, but his grandfather raised his hand to silence him.

"No harm done. This is the normal behavior of all dogs. Since the day of the council meeting, long ago, it is important that they smell each other's behinds."

He sat back, pensively, waiting for the young boy to respond. His dull eyes brightened, taking on a quizzical look, one which had not crossed his ancient face for a long time. Little Bear sat silently, waiting for the old man to continue. Finally, he could keep still no longer.

"What council meeting, *muchomes*?"

The sachem smiled, clearing her throat.

"I don't know if I should tell you this story. It might not sound so good for children's ears." He glanced slyly at the eager face of Little Bear.

"But didn't you hear it as a child, *muchomes*, like all the other stories you have told me?"

"This is true, my son. They did tell me this very story when I was but a child."

Little Bear sat back, attentively, happy that he had convinced the old man to continue. Black Turtle began his tale.

"You know how dogs smell each other when they meet. Well they are looking for something. Remember that all the dogs were related to the wolves long ago. Both the dogs and the wolves lived together. One winter day, the pack was getting very cold, so they sent one of their kind after some firewood so that they could build a fire to keep warm in the cold winter snow. This dog hunted high and low for a fire-stick, but could find none in the deep drifts, so he went to the camp of the Lenape to steal some fire sticks to take back with him to the camp of the dogs and the wolves.

When the dog arrived at the Lenape camp, the people were happy to see him and welcomed him into their lodges, petting him and feeding him. He was so glad to be treated so well by these people that he decided to stay with them. He forgot all about taking the fire sticks back to his pack.

The dogs and wolves waited and waited, but the dog never returned with the fire-sticks. After a while, they realized that he had left them for good, abandoned them, forsaken them all, dogs and wolves alike. This made the wolves very angry. A dog had lied to them, and soon the dogs and the wolves became enemies. The dogs and wolves parted company and went their separate ways, all because the dog had lied to the wolves."

Black Turtle paused, looking down at Little Bear sitting at his feet, cross-legged.

"Go on *muchomes*. Don't stop now! Tell me what happened after the wolves and dogs went their separate ways."

He drew a deep sigh, and with great deliberation, proceeded.

"From that day on, the wolves gave the dogs nothing but trouble, fighting and attacking them every time they ran into each other. So one day, the dogs decided to call a council meeting to see what they could do about the wolves. Before the meeting, the head of the pack made an announcement to all the dogs who came to the council meeting house.

'Remember that our council house is clean and holy and that we must not bring anything unclean into it.' Then he declared, 'From now on, when we meet in council, all you dogs must remove your *kekunemewoo* and place them in the basket at the door.'" Little Bear grinned.

"And this all the dogs did. They obeyed their lead dog and threw all their *kekunemewoo* into the basket and entered the council house to take their seats. Now, the leader of the pack, Long Dog, (he is called *chemingw* because of his long body), began to speak. We are told that he is the smartest of all the dogs. Well, *chemingw* stood up on his hind legs and asked each of his fellow dogs, we call them *mwekanewtuk*, to tell him what they had to say about the wolves.

This council meeting went on for a very long time since each dog had a different idea about what should be done with the wolves. Then, during one of the long speeches, suddenly a huge wolf head appeared at the door of the council house. As the wolf stuck his head in the door, all the dogs became very frightened and began to run out of the house, bumping into each other, knocking each other down as they tried to escape the wolves. The whole place was in confusion as all the dogs tried to squeeze through the entrance way at the same time.

They were in such a rush to get out of there, that as they ran by the basket at the door, each one grabbed the first *kekunemewoo* he touched, thinking it was his own. You see, there was such confusion that they grabbed any old one. When they got to the woods where they were safe from the wolves, each dog put on his *kekunemewoo*. It was only then that they realized that many of the dogs had grabbed the wrong one.

So you see, Little Bear, to this day the dogs are still sniffing around, looking for their own *kekunemewoo*. Our sachems tell us that this is the reason dogs smell each other's behinds. Each dog wants to be sure that the other doesn't have his *kekunemewoo*."

Black Turtle smiled broadly. Laughter soon filled the darkened, gloomy cabin.

"I must tell this wonderful story to my mother and father, Mechkalanne and Mockwasaka," announced Little Bear, as he stood up to leave the lodge, eager to repeat the story told to him by his grandfather.

"Thank you, *muchomes*. You are indeed a very wise man, as my father, Mechkalanne, has told me."

Little Bear left his grandfather's lodge, the two dogs tailing behind. He hurried across the abandoned village to one of the few cabins left standing, one that had not been consumed by a recent raid of the Pennsylvania militia. There he would find his little brother awaiting him.

Black Turtle's days were at an end. Early morning light found his clan standing before his hut, heads bowed. She Bear had summoned Mechkalanne and Mockwasaka to his side the night before. The old man's breathing had grown faint. The three stood beside the tired, old sachem, his body worn out. His eyes were closed, the lids fluttering. Suddenly, they opened wide, revealing two tiny beads of light, intense, but dwindling.

His lips, parched and cracked, whispered.

"Old woman, Mock, Mech. Come close!"

They drew closer to him, their ears bent to him. He drew in a long breath.

"White Turtle has called me to come to her. I must leave you. My spirit and your spirits are one now. Listen carefully to the earth and to the stars and to your dreams. Let the creatures which surround us lead the way.

They will tell you when it is time to leave and when it is safe for our people to cross over as they did in ancient times. It is the will of the Great Spirit, *Nanabush*, that I do not accompany you in this body. It is old and worn out, and I must leave it behind. My spirit will be with you always. Do not forget, Mechkalanne, Mockwasaka. You and Little Bear will lead our people safely to Ohio. You are the future of our people."

His eyes closed. He opened his lips, a crack, his voice dropping to a faint whisper.

"Do not forget my words. You are the future of our people. Listen closely to the earth and to its children in your dreams and in your waking moments. You will see my vision, hear my voice in the rush of the wind, the sounds of the night. Open your hearts to them when they beckon you. Answer their call. My dream vision has become your dream vision. Keep it alive."

Dawn found the trio huddled beside the dying man, their eyes closed, Mock's and Mech's fingers intertwined. They sat behind the old woman, her hands covering the old man's, their dark skin, paper-thin, folded together on his chest, barely lifting up and down.

She Bear's crooked body was hunched over the motionless figure, the back of her head shaking. Her soft weeping shook Mech out of her own troubled reverie. She had never seen this, her mother, cry, nor had she ever seen her own birth-mother in tears. Her thoughts turned back to Esther Tidd. The two women, one a sachem's woman, the other a squatter's wife, born into two worlds ages apart, bore so much hardship in silence.

Mock felt her own mortality, and that of her birth family. It was not just her adoptive father dying. It was Jacob Tidd as well. She reached gently out to touch the old woman's stooped shoulders. In the darkness, her shaking body faded into that of the dying sachem.

Mech tried to comfort the grieving women. He groped in the darkness, his arms halting. It was as if some ghost had appeared to him and was now slipping away, freeing itself from his grasp. His were the arms of the hunter, helpless before this enemy. He tried to make out the old man's form. It escaped his keen night vision, his silhouette growing fainter in the dim light, a shadow in the half-light of the pre-dawn hours.

His father's burden shrinking, Meck's broad shoulders sagged as if beneath a heavy weight. Suddenly, the sachem's body stiffened, his bony hands seizing She Bear's. His small deep-set eyes opened briefly, two tiny beads of light, barely visible, two distant twin stars in the night sky, deep in their nests of wrinkles; and then they closed. He was gone.

*   *   *   *

Weenee keeshooh—November. The November morning broke still and warm, the pine woods tinder dry. It had not rained since late summer and the parched forest bordering the Susquehanna stood witness to the fall drought. Complaining under foot, dry brush covered the forest floor. Summer foliage clung jealously to the oaks, birch, and maple, within a hawk's flight of the river and the abandoned Delaware village of *Shesequin*, where Black Turtle's clan remained. A few years earlier, a great flood had swept down the Susquehanna, and now drought had brought the clan to the verge of starvation.

Little Bear sat beneath an oak tree at the edge of a small clearing. The warm November sun splashed its gentle rays across the clearing, striking the nape of his neck. He sat half asleep, facing an incline crisscrossed by deer trails. At the bottom of the hill below him was a swampy hollow with a small spring at its center. It was a trickle now, the only watering hole for the deer herd which inhabited the woods. The deer, along with their Indian brothers, were suffering from the drought.

Mechkalanne, leaving Little Bear facing up the hill, had moved silently away, disappearing into the heavy foliage, making his way beyond the hill to his hunting blind to await the thirsty deer descending to the spring. He disappeared in a stand of pine at the top of the hill. Little Bear marveled at the lack of sound his father's moccasined footsteps made in the dry brush and leaves.

A tepid breeze wafted down the hill toward the boy. Mech knew that Little Bear sat downwind to any buck approaching the spring. A swatch of bright blue flitted through the green pine boughs—a silent jay bird. A lone chickadee landed on an oak limb for a brief stay, nervously cocking its brown bonnet cap at the youth. The little bird landed a hand's length from his crossed legs, its sharp little eyes blinking at him inquisitively.

Distracted by the languorous warmth of the late autumn day, Little Bear sat dozing beneath the oak. Suddenly a single shot rang out from across the hill in the direction of his father. Jumping to his bare feet, the boy ran, half stumbling, around the hill. He dragged his thin legs across the brush-covered incline, spotting the hunting blind, and beyond, his father's tall form, bent over a dark brown mass, the motionless hulk of a large buck, its rack of antlers clearly visible.

Breathless, the boy rushed up to the waiting marksman. Mech was chanting a prayer of thanksgiving, sighing in relief as he stared down at the animal. His son imitated his sigh. Their small clan would not go hungry this day. Mechkalanne reached for his leather belt, housing his deer knife.

He quickly dressed out the dead animal. The early afternoon sun was at its zenith in the southern sky. The heat still mounting, father and son each grabbed one of the gaunt animal's hind hooves, dragging it through the complaining dry brush to a pallet left at forest's edge. They placed the dead creature on the pallet.

"We must return to the cabin quickly, Little Bear, my son. Mock and She Bear will be most happy, glad to see us return with fresh deer meat. Their faces will be smiling with joy when they spot our kill. We will invite the others to feast with us."

When Mech and his son arrived at their cabin, Mock met them at the door. Her face lit up when she spotted the dead stag on the pallet the pair was dragging behind them. Tears came to her eyes.

"My husband, my son. I am proud to call you the great hunters you are."

She grabbed the two men, drawing them together in a single embrace.

"She Bear is too weak today to help us roast the deer meat. I know she is proud of her son and grandson."

Mock left the two hunters to skin out the buck while she reentered the cabin to share with She Bear the good news of the kill. Soon the dozen Delaware remaining in the deserted village, those who had not fled the militia, or had been driven away, gathered outside Mech's cabin to await the preparation of the venison for roasting.

A cooking fire was soon blazing before their cabin, deer meat turning on a spit which Mock had prepared for the feast. Darkness found the small clan devouring the skimpy steaks, wolfing them down as only the starving do. In the light of the blazing camp fire, their faces were gaunt and strained, revealing the unrelenting hunger that had dogged them since their arrival on the Susquehanna.

After they had had their fill, they leaned back to enjoy the unusual warmth of the November evening. Their bellies full, they were relishing a moment of tranquility in the midst of the storm of the American Revolution. They had watched the few remaining Indian peoples' camps in the valley destroyed by the invading militia, much like a few springs earlier, when their thatched huts had been torn apart and swallowed up by the invading waters of the flooding Susquehanna.

Driven back and forth by the battling militia, the long knives, and their Indian allies, the only refuge remaining was the Moravian missions further west. But Mechkalanne would have none of their Christian charity. As Black Turtle before him, he did not trust them.

Little Bear sat proudly between his parents. Suddenly his face fell. He grew sad.

"I miss Black Turtle and his stories. If he were still among us, I'm sure he'd have one of his wonderful tales to tell us even if it is not *Lawilowan*, and even if the lowly creatures that crawl upon and under the ground threatened us with their powerful medicine if we dared to tell such stories this night."

Mockwasaka cleared her throat. "There is one story She Bear told me when I first came to live among the Lenape."

"*Ktellinen! Linen*! Tell us!" each of the twelve cried out in turn.

Their eyes were on Mockwasaka as she began her tale, slowly, deliberately, rocking back and forth, the rhythm of She Bear's words breaking forth through her voice.

"It is right and good that this brief moment of joy and fulfillment remind us, as She Bear has taught me, that there was a time when men knew no joy such as that we share tonight. They had let their whole lives be devoured by work, hunting for food, then sleep, just to arise the next day to repeat this monotonous existence. They labored and slept, only to awake again to labor. Soon their minds softened and weakened. They began to rust away like the minds of lazy young braves who refuse to work or hunt for the good of their people.

During those days of boredom and monotony, when joy herself was absent, there was a man who lived near the Big Water, with his wife and two sons. They were proud, spirited young braves, all happy to become great hunters as their father before them. Even before they reached manhood, they did all kinds of daring activities to make themselves as strong as their huntsman father."

.Little Bear's thin chest swelled with pride.

"And their mother and father were happy, glad at the thought that the boys would provide for them when they grew old and weak. They would find food for them when they were too old to care for themselves."

She glanced back at the darkened cabin where She Bear slept.

"But one day when the eldest son went into the forest to hunt, he never returned that night. He had vanished without a trace."

Her listeners groaned, sighing collectively as she sat back, relishing their response. After a silence, she continued. Little Bear twitched his skinny legs nervously, impatiently.

"The boy's parents searched and searched for him, but it was all in vain. They found not a single trace of the missing hunter. Their parents grieved for their lost son and watched with fear as their second and youngest son went on the hunt for the first time. You can imagine how much they must have worried that he too would disappear as did his older brother.

This boy, who was named Only Son, liked to stalk deer; but his father preferred to take his canoe into the Big Waters to hunt sea creatures. As the boy grew in strength and skill, he was finally allowed to go inland and hunt as he pleased, while his father rowed to sea in his canoe. Parents, you know, cannot spend their whole life worrying about the safety of their children, even if it is their only son."

Mock smiled at Little Bear. He nodded.

"One day, Only Son, who was stalking his brother, the white tailed deer, looked up to see a mighty eagle circling overhead. As he pulled out an arrow to prepare to shoot at the great bird, it descended, finally settling on the ground not far from where he stood. It removed its feathered hood and turned into a young Lenape brave and began to speak to Only Son.

'I am the one who killed your brother, and I will kill you too unless you promise me that when you return to your village, you will arrange to hold a ceremony—a celebration filled with chanting and stomp dancing. Do you agree to do this or not?'

Only Son was more than glad to obey the eagle brave, but he had no idea what the words chanting and stomp dancing meant. He had never heard of such things.

So he asked the eagle, 'I would gladly do as you have commanded me, but what do you mean by chanting and stomp dancing? What is a celebration?'

'If you come with me, my mother will teach you the nature of such festivity. But you must listen to her and heed her directions. Your brother scorned these gifts we offered him. He would not listen, so I killed him. If you come with me, you will learn how to chant, and as soon as you learn to stomp dance, I will free you to return to your village and your people.'

Only Son announced, 'I will come with you,' and the two set off for the land of the eagles.

As they walked along together, Only Son looked up to see the young eagle brave turn into a big, strong man wrapped in shining eagle feathers. The two then walked a great distance, across mountains, along deep river gorges as they traveled further and further inland. Finally they came to the tallest mountain Only Son had ever seen and they began to climb it.

'Our lodge sits atop that mountain,' the eagle man said.

As the two approached the mountain crag, Only Son heard a throbbing noise which grew louder and louder until his body was vibrating to the sound coming from the crest of the mountain.

'Do you hear that thumping sound?' asked the eagle man.

'Yes, it is a deafening sound like nothing I've ever heard before.'

'That is the sound of my mother's heart beating.'

So the eagle man and Only Son came near the eagle's nest which was built on the highest mountain peak. Actually it was a house, like a man's dwelling, and not a bird's nest at all.

'Wait here, while I go to fetch my mother, White Eagle, so that I may alert her of your arrival.'

He disappeared into the house and soon returned to get Only Son. They entered a big room built like our own cabins, like the Big House of your father and grandfather back on the banks of the *Lenapewihituk*. There was a cot at the back of this eagle cabin, and there sat the young eagle's mother, old and feeble, her feathers all frayed and broken. She looked very sad."

Mock hesitated for an instant, glancing back to where the ailing She Bear lay. There was a hush among the Indians.

"The eagle man announced to his mother, 'Mother Eagle, I have brought you a brave who has promised to hold a festival of chant and stomp dance when he returns to his village. But he has told me that men have no idea how to chant and beat drums to a chant song's rhythm. They don't know how to enjoy pleasurable things and just have a good time, so this young brave has come with me up here to learn how to do these things.'

The tired old mother eagle lifted her feathered head and ancient beak. Her feeble eagle eyes lit up, beads of joy. Her son's words brought new life to her sad face.

'The first thing you must do is build a great log cabin, a Big House where many men and women may gather for *Gamwing*.'

So the Lenape brave and the eagle brave set to work building a great ceremony hall, a Big House, much larger and much finer than any cabin you see around here."

Mock glanced around at the deserted village cabins surrounding them, those that had not been burned by the militia.

"When the two braves had finished building the festival hall, the mother eagle taught them how to make a chant song, and how to bring this song up from deep within their throats. Then she made them a drum and taught them to beat it in rhythm to this deep song, and finally how to dance to its sounds and rhythms.

When the mother eagle had finished teaching the young brave all this, she said, 'Now before you can call your people to the Big House, to this feast hall for this wonderful celebration, you must call on the hunters to gather as much meat as they can to prepare for the *Gamwing* ceremony. During this time there will be periods of abstinence, so that afterwards all those assembled will require big feasts.'

'But I have never seen my people gather together in such a way. We have always traveled, worked, and eaten alone. We know of no other way.'

'Men know of no other way because they have not yet received the gift of joy. Do as I have told you. Build your celebration hall, your Big House. Make all your preparations as I have said. Once they are made, you will summon your people, men and women, to come to the Big House where you will meet them. Once you have gathered them all together there, invite them to come to participate in your celebration of chanting and stomp dancing. Remember that mankind is lonely and sad and they must be taught this gift of joy.'

When Only Son said farewell to his new eagle friend and returned to his village, he told his people about his adventure with the eagles and how they had given him a powerful gift to take pleasure in chant and stomp dance and how his heart now beat with this awesome gift of joy. His parents listened to his story, shaking their heads in disbelief. They could not imagine such a powerful gift as the eagles' because they had never experienced anything like it. But they dared not question his story, since they knew that if they did not heed the eagles' command, they might take Only Son from them.

A Big House was built, following the eagles' command, meat was gathered and prepared for the celebrants, fathers and sons combined words, words filled with joy and wonderment, which described their ancient memories and dream visions, which they set to a chant. They made drums to beat to their chants and give rhythm to their dance. Their spirits soon grew warm from the chants and their bodies from the stomp dancing. Laughter filled their lives and they began to see everything and everyone around them in a new light.

When the first celebration of *Gamwing* was finished, which lasted until morning light, and when all the couples had departed, Only Son and his parents realized that they and their people were not alone any more. They had never seen so much laughter and talking and so many people so carefree and joyous. They swore then and there that they would hold many celebrations from then on, that laughter and merriment would be a part of their lives and their peoples' lives, that they would commemorate with chanting and stomp dancing the eagles' gift of joy to their people at least once a year."

"And so the old mother eagle spared Only Son's life?" asked Little Bear.

"That she did," responded Mockwasaka, falling silent before her small audience.

The camp fire had died down into a heap of red hot embers, their glow illuminating the listeners' faces. Their bellies were full of deer meat, their troubled faces glowing and serene. Their hearts were glad and warm. The cold reality of the pillaged Delaware villages, of the warring bands of Indians, of the militia roaming up and down the Susquehanna, all was lifted away in this joyous moment.

Little Bear, his mind swimming with images from Mock's tale, decided that when they arrived in Ohio, when he became a strong brave like his father, Mechkalanne, he would gather together his people to celebrate *Gamwing* and the birth of joy.

On the Muskingum

Mechkalanne stood at the door of the cabin, his copper face blanched, eyes dulled, shoulders sagging. Beads of sweat studded his wide forehead, running profusely down his thick neck, gathering in a narrow river between his bare breast bones, smaller rivulets flowing off his hairless chest to join the main flow. Icy dread raced up Mock's back, rolled over her own shoulders, settling down in a fist of a knot in the middle of her stomach. The dread she had left behind on the trail to the Delaware was back.

She rushed to catch the man as he stumbled through the open cabin door. She hardly recognized him, like a stranger who had broken in to disrupt one of her rare moments of tranquility since they had taken refuge in this Moravian mission village on the Muskingum. His black, straight hair hung lifeless in dull clumps, its sheen, vanished.

"Mech! Mech! What has happened to you?"

Her voice trailed off. She choked. She pressed his hot face against her bosom. Like a fire brand it burned her flesh.

Mech had left the village two suns earlier in search of what little game the nearby Muskingum valley swamps might surrender to the starving Indians. She had not expected him back for at least two more suns, and now she was drawing from her own ebbing strength to support the big man as he crumpled into a heap at her feet. Screaming for Little Bear, asleep in the back corner of the cabin, little Bright Eyes at his feet, she managed to drag Mech's body to a small fur-covered cot in the far corner of the one room dilapidated cabin.

Little Bear was awake now and quickly slipped out of his coverlet, rushing to the side of his frightened mother. In the ten years they had been together, she had never seen Mech ill. An invisible force held him in its grip. She let his burning hands slip from her grasp, his body curling up in a ball on the cot at her feet.

She peered into the feverish eyes of the hunter. They did not respond to her questioning gaze. She turned Mech over, pulling his drenched shirt loose from his trousers, freeing his powerful legs from his baggy pants. She examined him from head to toe, searching for a wound, a hunting injury. His broad back heaved. The sweat poured from him producing a glistening sheen across his back, its copper tone a darker hue now.

She ordered the frightened Little Bear to run for help. There was a white man at the mission who practiced white man's medicine. Little Bear was to fetch him as quickly as possible. The breathless boy was gone in an instant. She looked down into the passive face of the unconscious man—her rock, her David, her life. Then a calm took hold of her. She glanced across the dimly lit cabin at the sleeping Shining Eyes, the infant serene, oblivious. Gathering her skirt's hem up around her waist, she grabbed a clay pot and ran out the open door to the nearby stream to draw cold water. She would swab Mech's fever-wracked body. She would fight this enemy with all her strength.

She returned to his side, the pot overflowing. Little Bear had not yet returned with the paleface medicine man. She found Mech on his stomach, the coverlet she had placed over him tossed aside. His convulsing body was rising and falling on the cot. She pulled her skirt off, dropping her undergarment to the dirt floor of the cabin. She ripped the cotton into long strips, plunging them into the cold water. Removing the rest of his clothes, her hands trembling, she gently placed the swabs across his back, chest, and legs. She felt the heat of the fever rising from his body each time her hand laid a new compress on him. He seemed smaller, thinner to her now as he lay at her feet, no longer the towering man whose boundless energy always amazed her.

The night passed and day came. And then a second night and day—and a third. Mock did not move from the side of Mechkalane who lay in a deep sleep.

The white medicine man arrived the following morning, examining the delirious Indian, careful not to touch his burning skin. He shook his head, turning to Mock.

"There is nothing we can do until the fever breaks. Pray for this noble man. He is in the fight of his life. I will summon one of the missionaries to come to minister to him."

He hurriedly left the cabin. He did not turn back to take a last glance at the sorrowful scene of the suffering Lenape hunter, his white woman at his side, his infant son asleep at the rear of the cabin. He shook his head sadly.

For three days, Mech fought the fever, at times in silence, others, his body writhing in convulsions. One night he awoke, pulled Mock to his side, and muttered in a strange, foreign tongue. She shivered as guttural tones emerged from deep within his throat. "It is I who killed your Rebecca Tidd. It is I who butchered her as her brethren did White Fawn, whom they took from me."

She looked away, horrified. Mech's face was twisted in a wild grimace. He had thrown the blanket from his perspiring body. He had shrunk terribly. A discoloration had spread over him. His head fell back, his torment abating some, and he fell into a deep sleep.

The following morning, Mock was startled awake. Mech was sitting up on his cot, soaked from his body fluids. His eyes were clear, the dullness gone. The fever had broken. She jumped to her feet, rushing to his side, trying not to break down in relief. A single sob escaped from her. As she approached the sick man, arching her body over his, reaching out to embrace him, she recoiled in horror. Flat, scarlet spots covered his face. She yanked the blanket from his body. The rash was visible on his neck and upper chest and arms. In a matter of hours, the spots spread over the rest of his chest, back, and legs, the rash denser on his face.

Throughout the following days, Mock watched the transformation of the handsome face and body of her David. The spots raised up into pimples, then pustules. The pustules burst, yellow puss oozing out. Mech's body was covered with so many puss pimples that its once copper hue turned an ugly yellow. The scourge was devouring his body, reeking a sickening odor—as if he were rotting away, she thought.

On the ninth day of the hunter's suffering, his entire body began to hemorrhage. Only his strength sustained him, extending his final breaths. Mock knew that his end was near. She no longer recognized his pox-ridden body. The paleface medicine man returned several times to examine the agonizing Indian, standing at a distance from him. He warned Mockwasaka to stand back from the dying man as well, removing Little Bear and Bright Eyes from the cabin. He knew that such a virulent pox could devastate the mission village if Mech were not isolated from the other Indians. They had witnessed the results of such an epidemic on the Big Island years earlier.

Mock sat quietly in her wicker chair, near the entrance to the crude cabin, her back to her husband, as if she were awaiting the arrival of a visitor. She rocked her aching body back and forth, praying for her husband's quick release.

"Almighty God, *Nanabush,* our One and Only God, our Creator. Deliver my Mechkalanne's soul from his ruined body."

She uttered the words over and over, first in Lenape, then in English.

"Lord have mercy on us, our Redeemer. *Nihillaliyenk ktemageleminen, Nihilla-peholkwenk.*"

Exhaustion overtook her, and she surrendered to another savior, sleep.

She awoke the following morning, bolting from the wicker chair. She rushed to the Indian's side. His face, chalk white, had regained its usual serenity. His dull, once shining, eyes were open, but Mechkalanne was no longer there. Mock froze. She stared at the lifeless body, then slowly withdrew. She covered her mouth. She wanted to scream out her grief. Yet she felt relief, a release. She thought of her brother, Aaron, and Rebecca, and the ugliness of their demise. So long as she lived, she would never come to understand why such good souls should have to suffer such hideous ends.

She went to leave the cabin, then turned back to look at Mechkalanne. She reached out to touch him, to kiss him, then withdrew her hands. She remembered the white medicine man's warning. She dared not touch him.

Mockwasaka knelt down before the silent Mechkalanne and said a prayer She Bear had taught her. "The earth is your mother, she holds you. The sky is your father, he protects you. Sleep, sleep, my Mechkalanne. Rainbow is your sister. She loves you, as does Mockwasaka. The winds are your brothers, they sing to you, as do I. Sleep, sleep, my Mechkalanne. We are together always. We are together always. There never was a time when this was not so. I love thee—*Kta-holell. Aptahowaltowagan*—Love unto death. Thy will be done."

She uttered her prayer over and over as she stumbled out of the cabin and through the mission village to retrieve her two sons.

1782

Little Bear lay on the moist bank, dropping his fishing line carefully into the swift current of the small stream. Shadows deepened, the depths of the creek barely visible in the fading afternoon light. The speckled trout lay an arm's length from the black line he was lowering into the whirling eddies. Foam, like soap suds, gathered around a blackened, water-soaked overhanging branch, brushing its sodden surface against the vortexes, dark dervishes caught in the midst of their frenzied dance.

Stretched out on his belly, he inched slowly to the edge, watching the rapid water carry the line downstream to a greenish black hole. It came to a halt in the center of the fishing hole, backed by an earthen bank. A giant night crawler, half of his serpentine body threaded on a white bone hook, struggled valiantly, its thin filament undulating in the swift current.

Little Bear leaned out over the water's surface. Naked except for a small loincloth, he wrapped his little feet and thin legs securely around the remains of a fallen tree trunk at water's edge. The powerful current had devoured its roots, a few blanched, scraggly ones remaining. His small head grazed the frenzied water, white bubbles of froth popping as they brushed against his little nose. His dark, almond eyes were fastened on the journey of the struggling worm, his sandy hair pulled back in a single braid, secured with a fish bone.

The worm was struggling halfway down the fishing hole, untouched by the wily trout. Little Bear's belly began to growl, reminding him of their plight. As his father before him, he always prayed to *Nanabush* and his *manitowuk,* a prayer his father had taught him. But he had forgotten to recite it before pitching his fishing line into the stream. And now not even a single strike!

Light in the darkening swamp faded quickly, and the boy, empty-handed, started back to reach the settlement before nightfall. He felt shame, knowing how disappointed Mockwasaka would be when he returned to their cabin with not even one small speckled trout to show for all his efforts. She depended on him now to secure their meager food supply for her and his little brother, Bright Eyes, now that Mechkalanne had been taken away by the Great Spirit, *Nanabush*, barely two springs earlier. She would be waiting at the cabin door, clutching Bright Eyes to her side, praying that his older brother would return with their dinner.

Little Bear darted through the swamp, enveloped in darkness, his sure feet following a worn footpath only he could tread on a moonless night. He recognized the cabin lights of the settlement, New Schoenbrunn, their eyes twinkling through the thinning cedar trees. He approached a tiny cabin standing at wood's edge, on the outskirts of the Moravian Delaware settlement.

The single eye of a dimly lit lantern revealed Mock sitting in her wicker chair, Bright Eyes asleep on her lap. Her face was thinner, more gaunt than the round face of Polly Tidd thirteen years earlier, her rosy complexion gone, now weathered, sun beaten. Her eyes were as blue as ever, but her skin was leathery, with small creases at her lips, crows feet at her eyes. Except for her red hair and blue eyes, she looked like an aging Indian woman. Mock spotted Little Bear, empty handed. Her face fell in a sadness, verging on despair..

Gnadennhuten— March 1783

Mockwasaka stuck out like a sore thumb. Her hair tightly braided, dressed in a loose fitting cotton dress, little Bright Eyes at her side, she labored among a group of Moravian Delaware gathering ears of corn from tattered stalks left untouched from the previous season's harvest. Men, women and children, (the men were working along side their women), were desperately picking the dried corn, keenly aware of the dangers threatening them from all sides.

The plantation was alive with activity as the Indian Christians gathered the corn in piles, bagging and storing in the nearby woods what they could not carry away. They were determined to finish the harvest, interrupted the preceding autumn by the British long knives and their Indian allies, Captain Pipe and his Munsey followers. They had forced the peaceful Indians to leave their villages, marching them to Sandusky. If they did not submit to them, they were told, they risked death at the hands of the American militia from Pennsylvania. And if they did not heed their demands, they threatened to arrest them all as spies for the Americans and remove them forcibly. The Delaware reluctantly agreed to follow their British captors back to Sandusky, to "Captives Town." A few stragglers, including Mockwasaka and her two sons, remained in the deserted village.

The Moravian Indians had spent the winter near starvation in "Captives Town." They finally convinced their British "hosts" and their Wyandot allies to let them return to the Muskingum and their mission towns to finish harvesting the corn.

Mock worked with the other Indians, listening to them discuss their plight—caught between the marauders (led by Captain Pipe, Simon Girty, the evil white renegade, along with their British allies), and the American militia men. The militia was seeking revenge for the murders and scalping of innocent settlers on the Western Frontier. She recalled Mech's distrust of the Moravians along with the British and American long knives, and here she was in their very midst, like her Christian brethren, caught between the two warring parties. She hated the thought of suffering the fate of the Moravians the preceding winter.

Gathering the few bags of corn she could carry back to their cabin in New Schoenbrunn, and with her toddler, Bright Eyes, half asleep, in tow, she pulled Little Bear aside.

"Listen carefully. We are in danger here. I am returning to the cabin with Bright Eyes. He is falling asleep standing up. Finish bagging your corn and follow us back to Schoenbrunn as quickly as you can. Do not stay with your friend, Thomas. He must return to Captives Town with his own people, and you must hurry back to the cabin before night fall."

"Yes, *Hase*. Yes, *Gawe*. I hear you. I will obey you."

Little Bear's eyes, downcast, told of his disappointment at his mother's command. It was his only chance to see his best friend, Thomas, who had returned from Captives Town with his clan. Thomas, standing in the next row, waved sadly to Mockwasaka as she disappeared through the woods in the direction of Schoenbrunn, the bulging sacks of corn still visible on her straining back. Bright Eyes toddled along beside her, his little hands clutching the hem of her dress.

Thomas and his family were working feverishly. He was taller than Little Bear, who had inherited his mother's stature and his father's physique. Their faces were the same dark copper.

Little Bear, in spite of his sandy hair, had the broad forehead and small piercing eyes of his father. Both youths' lean bodies were emaciated, their ribs sticking out through their white sweat-dampened cotton shirts. Thomas and Little Bear, in spite of their age, were grown men now.

Thomas' head bobbed up from the next corn row, spotting Little Bear standing, worried, watching his mother and little brother disappear in the direction of Schoenbrunn.

"Wait for me, Little Bear. We are but this one row from the end. I will accompany you back to your village to say goodbye to you and to your mother and brother before my family leaves for Captives Town."

Little Bear gathered the last ears of corn in a pile, placing them in the bag he carried in his buckskin belt, the only piece of Indian attire he wore.

"Hurry, *Ekhikuwet*, Talker, my friend. *Hase* as told me that we are in danger, exposed here in the open in this corn field. She has heard the rumors flying in Salem and Schoenbrunn that the Americans are nearby, eager for revenge for the slaying of their people in Pennsylvania."

The youths walked arm in arm as they prepared to return to the mission town, Little Bear's ears ringing with all the news that *Ekhikuwet* had to tell him since they had last seen each other the previous *tachwoak*. *Ekhikuwet* was Little Bear's *elongomat,* friend of friends. He had missed him during his absence. Dusk was fast approaching as they gathered the last ears of corn before leaving the cornfield.

Suddenly, a shot rang out from the nearby woods. Thomas and Little Bear dropped their bags of corn and ran toward the river bank in the direction of the shot. They entered the woods, men's voices rising from the far side of the Muskingum, barely visible through the trees.

Creeping through the brush, they stopped short of the river bank. They spotted a trough, halfway across the river, used by the Indians to gather maple sap for the sugar harvest. It had been commandeered by a dozen militia men, who were in the water, stripped naked, clinging to the trough which contained their clothing. Holding fast to their make-shift canoe with one hand, their teeth chattering, they paddled with the other. Another dozen men were standing on the near river bank awaiting the arrival of their comrades.

Little Bear and Thomas the Talker, recognizing the troops as militia men, slipped into a thicket and lay still. They spotted Joseph Schebosh, a half-breed Christian Indian, coming from the plantation in search of his horses. Two militia scouts, posted on the river bank, a man's stride from the stone-silent boys, spotted the approaching Schebosh. They ran towards him, their rifles raised.

Joseph threw his hands high in the air. He shouted to them in English.

"I am Joseph Schebosh, son of the white man, Mr. Schebosh!"

The one scout steadied his rifle, with a bead on Joseph's head. The other took a tomahawk from his belt, burying it in his forehead, tearing off his scalp.

The troops pressed on through the woods, their guns at their sides. They entered the plantation cornfield, raising their hands in a gesture of peace, signaling the alarmed Indians that they had come in friendship. One militia man stepped forward, his red face and fat jowls broken in a broad smile. He spoke in a loud voice to the startled Indians staring at him.

"We've come ta convey ya people ta Fort Pitt, where you'll be protected from th' British long knives who'r comin' ta destroy th' peaceful Delaware. There you'll be housed, clothed an' fed, safe from th' long knives warriors."

The hushed Delaware, setting aside their bags of corn, slowly responded to his offer, straggling one by one out of the cornfield and up to the edge of the woods, where they greeted the soldiers, extending their hands in welcome. Their silence was soon replaced by cries of welcome and relief.

Little Bear and Thomas the Talker, hidden in the bushes, watched helplessly, as a second group of militia, on horseback, set upon a lone Indian crossing the river, yanking the defenseless man out of his canoe, bludgeoning him with their tomahawks. The high water from the early spring freshet turned rust brown from the Indian's spilled blood. Jacob, Schebosh's son-in-law, who had been standing on the river bank tying up his corn sacks, dropped them and dove into the bushes, disappearing into a thicket, very close to the two boys. There he remained in hiding.

Night fell. The excited Delaware, guards surrounding them, walked slowly back to the mission village, where they spent the rest of the evening entertaining their visitors. Meanwhile, John Martin, a national assistant at the Gnadenhutten mission, spotted the tracks of shod horses on the western bank of the river. The Indian and his son lay on the top of a hill overlooking the village, where they watched the two peoples below exchanging friendly words.

Finally, his suspicions eased, convinced that the troops, led by Colonel Williamson, had come in peace, Martin turned to his son, ordering him to join the people in the village while he returned to Salem to spread the word that the Pennsylvania militia had come to deliver the Christian Indians. Later that evening, Martin arrived back in Gnadenhutten, informing Colonel Williamson that he had convinced the Salem Indians to place themselves under the colonel's protection, following him to Fort Pitt and safety as his men had promised.

Awaiting the arrival of the Delaware from Salem, Williamson and Martin sat together before the mission church, discussing the future of the Moravian Delaware.

"Some of the converts want to establish a branch mission at Fort Pitt. We could send to Bethlehem for new teachers and establish schools and churches of our own while our brethren on the Sandusky enjoy the ministry of our old teachers who were taken to Captives Town. What do you think of such a plan?"

Williamson nodded his head in approval. Turning to his aides, he raised the question of Martin's plan.

"What d'ya men think o' such a Christian undertakin?'"

They all smiled, feigning interest in the Indians' noble enterprise. In the meantime, Little Bear and Thomas the Talker slipped unnoticed into the crowd of Indians and militia men, aware of the white men's forked tongues, confused as to their motives.

The following morning, one of the militia's divisions headed for Salem town, where they summoned the remaining Delaware, convincing them to surrender their arms for safe keeping, setting fire to their town to prevent Indian and British troops from capturing it. They assured them that they would help them build another mission village as soon as they all arrived safely at Fort Pitt.

Returning to Gnadenhutten, the religious leaders proclaimed their profound faith in Christ and in his promises. Colonel Williamson addressed the crowd.

"Truly yer good Christian injuns!"

While the leaders of the two groups conversed, several boys, including Little Bear and Thomas, ran through the woods with the youngest of the militia, barely men themselves. They were teaching the American boys how to make bows and arrows. Little Bear and Thomas the Talker had no choice but to follow them. They knew if they tried to leave for New Schoenbrunn, they would suffer the same fate as Joseph Schebosh.

Arriving at the river bank where the butchery had taken place, the Delaware from Salem village, accompanied by a group of Williamson's horsemen, spotted a pool of blood and a bloody canoe on the sand at river's edge. They halted in mute surprise.

"Tie the'r hands 'hind the'r backs," shouted the leader on horseback.

The Indians, dumbfounded, submitted to the militia. They had surrendered all their weapons before leaving Salem village for Gnadenhutten with Williamson's men. Their hands bound, they were hustled across the river to join their brethren.

The Salem Delaware, now prisoners, stumbled along before the horsemen, approaching the center of Gnadenhutten where the chapel stood. Armed men stood guard before the two log cabins next to the chapel. They forced their captives to the ground before their cabins.

Moans and sobs rose from within. Soon Colonel Williamson galloped in on horseback, followed by his men on foot, all armed. He halted before the cabins, ordering his men to deliver their occupants to him.

"Get those red-skinned heathen out 'a ther' an' bring 'em here to join ther' cousins from Salem!"

The men burst into the cabins, driving out scores of moaning women and crying children from the first building, their men from the second. The soldiers quickly surrounded the crowd crowd of Moravian Delaware as they milled about in the small square before the chapel. When all the inhabitants of the two mission towns were rounded up, most of them women and children, and their hands tightly bound, the troops drew up in drill formation, forming a line of a hundred men facing the petrified Indians. They lay on the ground, cowering.

Williamson sat on a chestnut mount, his prominent chin sticking out, facing the huddled prisoners, ready to speak to them. Men on horseback flanked him on both sides. Behind them stood a line of foot soldiers, some dressed in makeshift military uniforms, identifying them as Pennsylvania militia, others in boots and flannels, farmers, who had just left their early spring plowing.

The colonel halted within a body's length of the Indians. He reached into his trouser's pocket, withdrawing a folded, wrinkled parchment. Flipping it open, he cleared his throat, and with an official air, he addressed the frightened crowd of Christian Delaware. Most of them did not understand English, since they had been taught the scriptures in German or in their Minsi dialect.

"Yer accused of aidin' th' British Injuns on the'r march to the American frontiers where they've massacred innocent men, women an' children. My men have examined yer horses. They're branded, provin' they've bin stolen from th' Americans. We've searched yer cabins an' found white men's clothin', tea kettles an' kitchen implements, children's caps an' toys, more ev'dence that you've raided settlers' homesteads an' carried off these items. What have ya ta say fer yerselves?"

There was silence among the stunned crowd. They did not understand the colonel's words. Finally, an older man, one of the two dozen men in the crowd, stood up, and with his hands tied behind his back, approached the colonel. He looked up at Williamson, his face grave, his jaws clenched, his long flowing hair, speckled with grey. As he spoke, his eyes cast up and down the ranks of the militia men. They looked away when his eyes met theirs.

"My name brother Abraham. I speak for these men, women and children, who cannot speak. We peaceful people. We wish you no harm. We have meant to be left alone to worship our God here with our teachers taken away by long knives to Captives Town. You wrong believing lies of brethren. Lenape people at Salem and Gnadenhutten, not enemies. Your enemies, Mingos, Wyandots, Shawnees join long knives *ingelischman*. Lenape peace-loving. We neutral, here in little Christian towns."

Williamson, facing brother Abraham, looked away.

"Finish yer' speech, Abraham. Get on with it, injun!"

He turned, shouting to his men.

"Listen close ta this savage's words. I want ya men ta decide if he's tellin' th' truth o' not.

He turned back to the Indian, scowling. Abraham continued.

"Many times we help Americans, give shelter when they pass through villages. We give same to *ingelischman* indians, if not, we die. War parties, we beg go back to Sandusky and Detroit. We give provisions to Colonel Brodhead and militia who pass through here. We no longer savages. We adopt ways of white men. We use utensils and instruments to cook and farm. Moravian teachers show us. We grow corn. We keep cabins clean and orderly."

Suddenly, a wild-eyed militia man came running from one of the nearby cabins, a woman's blood-stained dress in his hands. He sobbed, shaking his clenched fists at the crowd of Delaware, his face twisted in rage.

"It's Mary's dress! It's my Mary's dress! One of these savages killed my Mary!!"

"Mr. Wallace!! Han' me that dress. Han' me that dress!!"

The colonel grabbed the garment from the distraught farmer, waving it over his head.

William Wallace fell to the ground, his body writhing, as if he were suffering a fit.

"They butchered my Mary and my children, Joseph, Daniel, and my wee Anna. I found her poor little body impaled—her head twisted toward the settlements, her belly facin' injun country."

"Ther ya have it, Mr. Abraham!"

Williamson threw the bloody dress at the feet of brother Abraham. He turned to his men.

"What more proof do we need? I leave ta ya men ta decide. What'll we do with these murderin' heathen injuns?!"

William Wallace lifted himself up off the ground, his body no longer shaking. He screamed, crazed.

"Scalp 'em! Scalp 'em! Vengeance is mine, saith the Lord! Kill ever' last one of 'em!"

"Aye, aye," came a single voice from the militia men.

Williamson turned to his officers.

"It's up ta us officers ta decide. Shall we take these heathen pris'ners ta Fort Pitt or shall they be put ta death?"

One by one they dismounted. Finally the red faced lieutenant, who had convinced the Delaware to leave their corn field and accompany them to the mission, stepped forward.

"Let's put it to the men. It's they and ther families who've bin sufferin' at the hands of these savages."

"Aye, aye," came a single voice from the detachment. "Let the men decide."

Williamson shouted, "Agreed! Let th' men decide ther fate."

Facing the soldiers, the colonel ordered the assembled militia to form a single line, a hundred yards long. His orders were quickly followed, and when the men had drawn up in the line, he put the question to them.

"Shall th' Moravian Injuns be taken pris'ners ta Pittsburgh, o' put ta death? All in favor o' sparin' ther lives advance ta th' front o' th' line an' form a second rank."

The soldiers glanced to each side, quizzing the faces of their comrades, which moved down the line like a row of falling dominos. Restless, agitated, sheepish, the men kept looking back to their rear, as if some force behind them would help them decide the fate of the Moravians. Williamson shouted.

"Ya men have one minute ta make up yer minds. Step forward if ya want th' Moravians spared."

He returned to his mount, trotting up and down the line of soldiers, counting the handful of men who had stepped forward, each of them glancing backwards to see if any of his comrades were following him. There were none. Only a dozen men had formed a second rank.

The colonel returned to his post at the center of the line of militia men.

"Th' men have decided. The Moravian Injuns'll be put ta death at dawn. Choose th' means o' ther execution!"

The militia men remained silent.

A man came up from the rear, shouting.

"Set fire to ther houses an' burn 'em alive!"

It was William Wallace.

One of the men who had stepped forward to announce his opposition turned to face Wallace.

"How can we execute a bunch of fellow Christians, most women and children? These people have done us no harm. They're obviously not the murderin' red skins we're lookin' fer!"

A second voice rose from the crowd.

"Let's scalp 'em and take ther scalps home ta show as proof we've defeated the enemy."

The men were growing impatient.

A few shouted, "Aye, aye," and then there was silence broken from time to time by the sobs of the frightened women and the crying of children, huddled before them.

Williamson turned to the Indians to announce their fate.

"Ya people will be put ta death tomorrow at dawn by tomahawk. Return them ta ther cabins!"

He goaded his horse and galloped off.

A second militia man, who had stepped forward from the line, hung his head. He wrung his hands. He shouted out to the men who were herding the Moravians back into their cabins, the men into the first one, the women and children into the second.

"As God is my witness, I'm innocent o' the blood of these harmless Christian Injuns."

When Abraham and the other leaders of the Moravian Delaware at Gnadenhutten understood the decision of the Pennsylvania Militia from Westmoreland County, they informed their followers, crowded into the two cabins, of their impending deaths. Wailing and sobbing followed. As night fell, voices in praise and prayer rose from the darkened cabins surrounded by the militia. Christian hymns followed, first from the women's and children's cabin, filled to overflowing. Male voices sang in response from the other cabin. The voice of the Mohican, Abraham, rose above them all.

"Dear brethren. Our time to meet the Savior comes. Our end is near. You know I am a bad man. Yet to him I belong, as bad as I am. He will not reject me. He will forgive us all. I will hold fast to him to the end, though I am a great sinner."

His words were repeated over and over throughout the long night of the seventh of March, 1783. Early on the morning of the eighth, as they continued to sing hymns and exchange words of faith and consolation, the Moravians were led by a half dozen men to two adjacent cabins, one for the men, the second for the women and children, among them, Thomas the Talker and his family.

"Bring 'em ta th' slaughterhouses."

A shrill voice echoed through the empty streets of Gnadenhutten.

Earlier the previous evening, as the Christian Delaware were rounded up, the soldiers captured Thomas, dragging him off with the others. He and Little Bear had remained on the outskirts of the town with the youngest members of the militia. Little Bear, however, had spotted the approaching soldiers before they noticed him, and creeping into the bushes, he remained there without budging, the entire night, listening to the cries and the singing of the condemned Moravians. He shivered in the cold of early March, grieving the loss of his friend, Thomas the Talker, wondering if he would ever get back to Schoenbrunn to see his mother, Mockwasaka, and his little brother, Shining Eyes.

He prayed, his eyes tightly closed, that his mother and brother be spared, that they not be discovered by Williamson and butchered with the rest.

The execution of the Moravian Delaware was carried out by a handful of troops. Most of the militia withdrew in disgust. The first to die was Mr. Abraham, the Mohican. One of the militia spotted his long, flowing hair.

"It'll make a fine scalp!"

Mr. Wallace began the slaughter. He grabbed a cooper's mallet.

"This'll do just fine."

Beginning with Abraham, he drove the mallet again and again into the bowed heads of fourteen men, who fell before him. They were then scalped by two other soldiers. His face spattered with blood, Wallace handed the mallet to his comrade.

"My arms fail me. You continue. I think I've done pretty well."

Besides the mallets, they used Indian tomahawks, scalping knives, war clubs, and spears to carry out the execution. When the Delaware men and boys were dead, the women and children were led two by two to their executioners in their own slaughterhouse. The first women to die were two widows named Judith and Christiana. Christiana, who spoke German and English, fell to her knees before Colonel Williamson, her dark face twisted in terror, begging him to spare her life.

"I cannot help you."

Ninety Moravian Delaware died in the two slaughterhouses, besides those killed on the outskirts of the settlement—twenty-nine men, twenty-seven women, and thirty-four children. After burning the mission town of Gnadenhutten, the borderers returned home to Pennsylvania with ninety-six scalps on their belts. They were welcomed as heroes by many of their people, just as Possum Eater and his band had been fourteen years earlier. And they disappeared into the wilderness much like Possum Eater.

Only one Indian escaped the butchery as the men and older boys were being led two by two to their slaughterhouse. He had loosened and then slipped the bonds from his hands, so that he received only one blow from the mallet by the men, who then took his scalp, leaving him for dead. When he came to, he found himself lying at the bottom of the slaughterhouse, underneath a heap of bleeding corpses, his head bathed in blood. It was Thomas the Talker.

Thomas spotted one of his brethren, a boy named Abel, moaning, trying to raise himself up above the carnage. Thomas lay back, motionless, as one of the militia men entered the cabin cellar. Observing Abel trying to get up, he slammed his mallet into the boy's skull, splattering his brains over Thomas. Throughout that day, Thomas lay still in the heap of corpses in the cellar, in a bath of blood, as the slaughter continued above, the blood of the victims penetrating the floor, running in streams into the cellar below. He barely budged in spite of a hideous pock-marked face staring wide-eyed and lifeless, directly into his. It was the beheaded remains of Possum Eater.

At nightfall, the militia torched the slaughterhouses along with the entire village of Gnadenhutten. Thomas the Talker lay still until dark, then freed himself from the heap of mangled corpses. Bleeding profusely, he dragged himself through a narrow window, scooted across the ground into the neighboring woods, and to safety, as flames consumed the cabins.

It was late evening. Mock stood in front of her cabin in the smoldering ruins of New Schoenbrunn. It was one of the few huts that had not been torched by Williamson's troops as they passed through the village, intent on finishing the job they had started at Gnadenhutten. But the inhabitants of her village had been warned of the arrival of the troops.

Two Delaware had spotted them the first night as they approached Gnadenhutten, and the remaining Indians fled the village. Mock and Bright Eyes spent the day of March 8, hidden in the bushes near the cabin, her hands covering her child's mouth and curious eyes. Creeping out of the woods at twilight, she saw an orange glow in the sky to the south on the lower Muskingum. It was the burning village of Gnadenhutten.

Little Bear had not returned. She held Bright Eyes tightly.

"What ever shall I do? What ever shall become of us?"

In the pitch black, illuminated occasionally by a flaring ember from the dying ashes of one of the torched cabins, she spotted a grey shadow approaching her.

"*Gawe, hase*, Mockwasaka. It is I. Little Bear."

The voice resembled Mechkalanne's, only higher. She set Shining Eyes on the ground behind her. Two strong, smooth hands reached out from the darkness and took hold of her weather beaten ones.

For a split second she thought it was Mechkalanne who had returned to her. She collapsed into the arms of Little Bear. His trousers and shirt were covered with dirt and blood. She held on to his skinny body, as if she were hanging on to life itself.

* * * *

Mock's days living in the ruins of New Schoenbrunn, Ohio, were numbered. The American militia roamed unhindered throughout the region, their British counterparts nearby. She had picked enough corn at Gnadenhutten to last them a few months, but the valley of the Muskingum was devastated by the attacks, the game animals, along with their human brothers, gone. She dared not leave the cabin for fear of exposing her little family to the American militia, pursuing the British Indians up north, towards Sandusky.

One night, she and her two boys lay in silence on the cabin floor, underneath a blanket, as the troops camped a few yards away. After the destruction of the original village of Schoenbrunn years earlier, most men, red and white alike, avoided the village like the pox. New Schoenbrunn had since inherited the reputation of the original Moravian town. It was thought to be haunted by the spirits of the massacred Delaware Christians. War parties hurried by the ruins in fear and in awed respect.

But that night, a thunderstorm struck shortly after the troops, exhausted from their long march to Sandusky and back, had settled down to sleep. One of the men awoke and spotted in the sky, illuminated by constant flashes of lightning, an apparition. It was a horrible witch, trailed across the heavens by the skeletons of the murdered Indians of Gnadenhutten. As the storm beat down on them, unabated, the men rose before dawn and fled the village in terror.

Mock was relieved, but she knew they would return. She knew the Indian marauders would never set foot in the village. Once, at New Salem, she had heard that, returning from a raid of vengeance against the long knives on the Virginia frontier, a band of Delaware, with their cousins, the Shawnee, had stopped at the Big Spring nearby for a drink, the scalps and tongues of their victims hanging from their war belts. As they leaned over the edge to take a drink, they saw the reflection in the water of the murdered white men. Then suddenly, the dried tongues hanging from their belts began to wag, wailing and shrieking. The Indians fled, never to return to the ruined village.

A month after the massacre, while Little Bear was hunting in the woods a hundred yards from the cabin, two horsemen appeared, grabbing him, dragging the struggling youth to the village center where they were about to put him to death. Mock heard Little Bear's cries for help as she stood watch at the cabin door. The mounted soldiers had drawn their swords, and were preparing to dispatch Little Bear, pinned to the ground under the hoof of one of the cavalry horses.

She tore out of the cabin, her hair flying, knocking Bright Eyes on his behind, who tumbled out of the cabin behind her. A wildcat, she flung herself across the back of the startled horseman, grabbing the man's bare head, scratching at his eyes, trying to knock his raised sword from his hands. During the struggle, she landed on the ground next to Little Bear. Rolling across the ground, she covered her child's body with her own.

Staring defiantly into the surprised faces of the cavalrymen, she spit out in English.

"Kill me! Kill me!"

The two horse soldiers, taken aback, dismounted.

"Well, I'll be! What do we have here?"

"A white woman, me thinks."

"Less take her an' th' two boys ta Colonel Levine at Fort Pitt. He's ordered us not ta harm any white slaves we capture on our raids."

"Those two boys sure look like injuns to me."

Mock heaved a sigh of relief as she stood before her two sons, hiding their dark faces from the sight of the curious militia men.

"Where ya from, woman?"

She did not respond. She thought for a second. For an instant she could not remember where she was from.

"Canopus Hollow."

"Oh, so ya do speak English!! Where's Canopus Holler?"

"I don't know."

The covered wagon, drawn by a team of cavalry horses, a militia man on the buckboard, bounced down the mountain trail, Mockwasaka, Little Bear, and Shining Eyes peering out the back, their legs dangling from the rear of the wagon. The Highlands fell away behind them, the rough road giving way to a level, worn, stone covered one. She spotted a cabin in a small clearing, then another. They reminded her of the Tidd homestead, with its sloping roof and front stoop, it seemed a lifetime ago. Soon a half dozen cabins appeared on both sides of the road, a small pond in the background.

"Stop the wagon," she yelled to the driver. "I think this is it." She mumbled, "I remember it much bigger."

"You were sayin', ma'am?"

"Never mind. That must be Canopus Pond. Stop the wagon!"

The cavalry man reined in the team as Mock jumped from the still-moving wagon, her two sons hopping off after her. Taking the boys by the hand, she walked slowly towards the cabins, mesmerized.

"Goodbye," she whispered half to herself as she led the two boys away.

She glanced back at the retreating wagon, its load lighter, bouncing back up the mountain trail towards the Hudson.

Most of the forest and swamp had been cleared, the distant Highlands visible. She watched the wagon disappear. Spotting a farmer leading a yoke of steers up the road, dragging a load of logs, she signaled him to stop. The dust clearing, she yelled out.

"Is this Canopus Hollow"

"Canopus what?"

"Canopus Hollow!"

"No ma'am. This is Pecksville! That ther' yonder is Canopus Pond. Never heard of no Canopus Holler."

He eyed the dark-skinned children.

"Those half-breeds ya got ther?"

Mock pulled her two sons close to her side.

"Never mind."

The man was gone in a cloud of dust left by the team and the log-filled cart.

She walked slowly down the trail, her eyes searching for a familiar sign, the boys wandering nearby.

"It has to be here. It can't just have vanished off the face of the earth. Pa worked too hard to build the homestead and the stockade."

Suddenly, a sharp bird cry shook her out of her reverie. Looking up into the clear blue sky, she spotted a large red hawk circling over a small hill a few yards further down the trail.

She whispered, "Mechkalanne!"

"Come quick, my sons. Follow me!"

She hurried in the direction of the circling bird. She spotted a broken down cabin long since abandoned, the front stoop partially collapsed, a few rotting poles all that remained of a stockade fence.

She ran towards the ruined cabin, stumbling, looking up, searching for the hill in the back with the boulder at the top. Then she spotted it. Aaron's bright face flashed before her. Slowly, reverently, taking her son's hands, she dragged herself up to the top of the hill. They came to a halt before three weathered gravestones. She recognized the faded names of Aaron, Jacob, and Esther etched on the crude markers. Her skinny, callused index finger brushed each fading letter, carefully following its outline. She fell to her knees before the tombstones. She wept softly.

"What is this place, *gawe*? Is this our new home?"

Little Bear pulled on her sleeve. Bright Eyes imitated his older brother.

Mockwasaka grabbed her two sons, gathering them into her arms, pointing to the ruined homestead.

"Yes, Little Bear. We've found our new home. This place is *Winachk Hacki*, Sassafras Land!"

WORKS CONSULTED

Bierhorst, John. A Cry from the Earth: Music of the North American Indian. New York: Four Winds Press, 1979.

Bierhorst, John, ed. Four Masterpieces of American Indian Literature. New York: Farrar, Straus and Giroux, 1974.

Bierhorst, John, ed. In the Trail of the Wind: American Indian Poems and Ritual Orations. Farrar, Straus and Giroux, 1971.

Bierhorst, John. Mythology of the Lenape. Tuscon: The University of Arizona Press, 1995.

Bierhorst, John, ed. On the Road of Stars: Indian American Night Poems and Sleep Charms. New York: William Morrow and Company, 1994.

Bierhorst, John, ed. The Sacred Path: Spells, Prayers & Power Songs of the American Indians. New York: William Morrow and Company, 1983.

Bierhorst, John, ed. The Way of the Earth: Indian America and the Environment. New York: William Morrow and Company, 1994.

Bierhorst, John, ed. The White Deer and Other Stories Told by the Lenape. New York: William Morrow and Company, 1995.

Bliss, Eugene F., ed & transl. Diary of David Zeisberger: a Moravian Missionary among the Indians of Ohio. Vol. 1. Cincinnati, Ohio: Robert Clarke & Co., 1885

Booth, Russell H. Jr. The Tuscarawas Valley in Indian Days: 1750-1797. Cambridge Ohio: Gomber House Press, 1994.

Brinton, D.G., ed. Library of Aboriginal Literature. Vol. V: The Lenape and Their Legends. New York: AMS Press, 1969.

De Schweinitz, Edmund. The Life and Times of David Zeisberger. Philadelphia: J.B. Lippincott & Co., 1870. Reprint Edition: New York: Arno Press & The New York Times, 1971.

Donehoo, Dr. George P. Indian Villages and Place Names in Pennsylvania. Reprint. Bowie, Maryland: Heritage Books, Inc., 1992.

Drake, Samuel G. Indian Captivities or Life in the Wigwam. Auburn, New York: Derby and Miller, 1851 Reprint. Bowie, Maryland: Heritage Books, Inc., 1995.

Earle, Alice Morse. Customs and Fashions in Old New England, 1983. Reprint. Bowie, Maryland: Heritage Books, Inc., 1992.

Eisenberg, Leonard. Paleo-Indian Settlement Pattern in the Hudson and Delaware River Drainages. Occasional Publications in Northeastern Anthropology. Department of Anthropology, Franklin Pierce College. Peterborough Transcript: Peterborough, New Hampshire, 1978.

Gnadenhutten Monument Society. A True History of the Massacre of Ninety-six Christian Indians at Gnadenhutten, Ohio. New Philadelphia, Ohio: The Ohio Democrat, 1870.

Harrington, M.R. The Indians of New Jersey: Dickon Among the Lenapes. New Brunswick, New Jersey: Rutgers University Press, 1994.

Heckewelder, Reverend John. History, Manners, and Customs of the Indian Nations: Who Once Inhabited Pennsylvania and the Neighboring States. Memoirs of the Historical Society of Pennsylvania. Vol. XII. Reprint. Bowie, Maryland: Heritage Books, Inc., 1990. Highwater, Jamake. Legend Days. New York: Harper & Row, 1984.

Hitakonanu'laxk (Tree Beard). The Grandfathers Speak: Indian American Folk Tales of Lenape People. New York: Interlink Books, 1994.

Hopkins, Donald R. Princes and Peasants: Smallpox in History. Chicago: The University of Chicago Press, 1983.

Http://www.ilhawaii.net/-stony/lore28.html. "Blessed Gift of Joy is Bestowed Upon Man." Indian American Lore.

Kraft, Herbert C. and John T. The Indians of Lenapehoking: The Lenape or Delaware Indians. South Orange, New Jersey: Seton Hall University Museum, 1997.

Lawyer, J.P. Jr., B.S. History of Ohio from the Glacial Period to the Present Time.

Akron, Ohio: The New Werner Co., 1912.

Light, Richard, The Four Stones of Pecksville.

Lohrman, H.P. & Romig, Ralph H. Valley of the Tuscarawas: A History of Tuscarawas County. Dover, Ohio: The Ohio Hills Publisher, 1972.

McCutchen, David. Translator and Annotator. The Red Record: The Wallam Olum: The Oldest Indian American History. Garden City Park, New York: Avery Publishing Group, Inc., 1993.

Olmstead, Earl P. David Zeisberger: A Life among the Indians. Kent, Ohio: The Kent State University Press, 1997.

Olmstead, Earl P. Moravian Missions in North America: 1740-1821 1988.

Ruttenber. E.M. Indian Tribes of Hudson's River to 1700. 1872. Reprint. Saugerties, New York: Hope Farm Press and Book Shop, 1992.

Sipe, C. Hale. The Indian Wars of Pennsylvania. Reprint. Lewisburg, Pennsylvania: Wennawoods Publishing, 1995.

Stickney, Charles, E. A History of the Minisink Region. Middletown, New York: Coe Finch & I.F. Guiwits, Publishers, 1867. Reprint.

Tantaquidgeon, Gladys. Delaware Indian Medicine Practice and Folk Beliefs. Harrisburg, Pennsylvania. Pennsylvania Historical Commission, 1942. Reprint. New York: AMS Press, 1980.

Tuscarawas County Genealogical Society. The History of Tuscarawas County, Ohio. Reprint. Strasburg, Ohio: Gordon Printing, 1975.

Van Buren, Augustus H. A History of Ulster County under the Dominion of the Dutch. Astoria, New York: J.C. & A.L. Fawcett, Inc., 1989.

Virtue, Ross M. A History of Ganadenhutten: 1772-1976.

Wallace, Anthony F.C. King of the Delawares: Teedyuscung 1700-1763. Syracuse, New York: Syracuse University Press, 1996.

Weslager, C.A. The Delaware Indians: A History. New Brunswick, New Jersey: Rutgers University Press, 1990.

Weslager, C.A. The Delaware Indians Westward Migration. Wallingford, Pennsylvania: The Middle Atlantic Press, 1978.

Zeisberger, David, & Whritenour, Raymond. A Delaware-English Lexicon of Words and Phrases. Butler, New Jersey: Lenape Texts & Studies, 1995.